THE HELENA ANCHOR CROSS

Richard G. Edwards

Copyright 2015 by Richard G. Edwards

ISBN 978-0-692-49301-4

Published by EMTCC, LLC, Lexington, Kentucky

Printed in the United States of America on acid-free paper.

The characters and events in this book are fictitious. Any similarity to real persons, living or dead, is coincidental and not intended by the author.

EMTCC, LLC
2015

First Edition

Cover Photo

The photograph on the front cover, taken by the author on March 8, 2011, is of Jerusalem, Israel photographed from the Mount of Olives.

Acknowledgements

My wife, Carolyn, and several friends graciously agreed to review the manuscript of this book and offer suggestions and corrections. I am truly grateful to them for taking the time to do so. In addition to Carolyn (aka Carolyn Potter), Dr. Bill Green (aka Trigger Green), Drs. Carl and Gus Peters (aka Dr. Randy Peters), and Jack Sterling (aka Sheriff J. Bert Sterling) were the reviewers.

The original idea for the Anchor Cross theme came from the symbol used by my church, Anchor Baptist Church in Lexington, Kentucky. The book layout is the expert work of Mrs. Kelly Elliott. My sincere thanks to all!

Dedication

I would like to dedicate this book to Anchor Baptist Church and to the people of Harlan, Kentucky.

Anchor Baptist Church of Lexington, Kentucky was founded in 2000. My wife Carolyn and I became members there about a year later. The church uses as its symbol the Anchor Cross, as referenced in Hebrews 6:19, *'We have this hope (meaning salvation through Christ) as an anchor of the soul, sure and steadfast'*. It was from this symbol that I got the idea for the theme of my books. The current ministers at the church are Dr. Carl Peters, Senior Pastor, Dr. August Peters, Assistant to the Pastor, and Chris Keener, Associate Pastor for Student and Family Ministry. They have truly been very effective anchors for the souls of me and my family, and for all its congregation. My eternal thanks!

I grew up in Harlan, Kentucky. After spending the first 18 years of my life there, I left to begin college at the University of Kentucky in Lexington in 1958. I still have many friends and a few relatives living in Harlan. I have a lifetime of fond memories about the beautiful little town situated in the Appalachian Mountains of Eastern, Kentucky. I always enjoy my frequent visits there. My books have contained a lot of the stories and memories from Harlan that I will never forget. You'll find no better people anywhere. Pax Tecum!

Preface

If you have read either of my previous two books, **The Anchor Cross** (now also available as **The Anchor Cross Second Edition**) or **The Pelle Anchor Cross**, you are aware that the theme of the books revolve about six anchor crosses that were cast by Roman Emperor Constantine the Great in 325 A.D. using gold that was traced back to being blessed by my Lord Jesus Christ and then given to Saint Peter to help start the church. **The Helena Anchor Cross** continues with that theme.

I would encourage my readers to share their thoughts and comments with me.

My email address is: richardglennedwards@gmail.com

If you would like copies of either or both of my first two

books, please either contact me at the above email address, or you may order them from:

www.BookLocker.com   *The Anchor Cross*
www.Amazon.com   *The Anchor Cross,*
The Anchor Cross Second Edition, The Pelle Anchor Cross
www.BarnesandNoble.com   *The Anchor Cross,*
The Anchor Cross Second Edition, The Pelle Anchor Cross

May God Bless, and Pax Tecum!

Richard G. "Dick" Edwards

Lexington, Kentucky 2015

Chapter 1

Rome, Italy

326 A.D.

Helena sat alone in her chamber. She had dismissed her servants, and wanted time alone to reflect on the trip upon which she was about to embark. Tomorrow she would leave Rome to travel to Palestine . . . to Jerusalem. Approaching the age of 80, she knew it would be a very difficult trip for her physically. But it was one she had to make. She was determined to locate the true cross. The cross upon which her savior, Jesus Christ, had died for the sins of mankind. And after finding the cross, she would establish a church at that location so that future generations would always remember the story of

Calvary. She also planned to visit the sites of Christ's birth and ascension, and to establish churches at those locations as well. Very lofty goals. And she was old. But she was determined.

Helena had been a Christian all her adult life. She was a true believer, and had studied Christ's life and teachings. In 272 A.D. she gave birth to a son, Constantine, who in 306 A.D. became Emperor of Rome, a position he held for some 31 years until his death in 337 A.D. It is known that Helena's Christianity was accepted at some point by her son Constantine. Prior to 313 A.D. the Roman Empire worshiped idols. In 313 A.D. Constantine and Licinius issued the Edict of Milan decriminalizing Christian worship, and Constantine declared himself a Christian. From this time forward, Christianity could be practiced in the Roman Empire without persecution. Constantine became a great patron of the Church and frequently consulted with Pope Sylvester I concerning Christian matters.

Around 325 A.D. Constantine had a vision that lead him to produce a symbol that would become associated with Christianity. Prior to this time, and going back well before the birth of Christ, the primary symbol associated with religion was the anchor. Christ died on the cross, a death reserved for only the very worst criminals. But Constantine was determined to make the cross the primary symbol for Christianity, and in his vision he saw a symbol that combined the anchor and the cross. One that would provide continuity from religions of the past, symbolized by the anchor, to Christianity, symbolized by the cross. He gathered artists, described to them his vision, and commissioned them to draw his envisioned anchor cross. Constantine then selected his favorite from among the drawings and presented it to his best metal formers and directed them to produce a mold into which would be poured gold to produce the anchor cross. Constantine had consulted with Pope Sylvester I about his vision and interest to produce the anchor cross. After hearing the story, the Pope told Constantine that he would contribute a bar of very special gold for the anchor cross. The Pope said that this bar of gold was one of many held by the church that had their origin traced back to the time of Christ. He said the gold bars, called St. Peter's gold, had been blessed by Christ and then given to St. Peter to help start the church. Constantine graciously accepted the one bar of St. Peter's gold, and his metal formers were then able to melt it to produce six of the golden anchor crosses. These became known as the "Savior's Crosses". Constantine was very pleased with the beautiful, priceless Savior's Crosses. He kept only one for himself, and presented the other five to Pope Sylvester I to be distributed as determined by the church.

Helena thought about her meeting yesterday with Pope Sylvester I. The Pope had been informed about Helena's upcoming trip to Jerusalem, and the purpose of her trip. At their meeting Helena and the Pope discussed the trip, and then the Pope surprised Helena by giving her one of the Savior's Crosses and asked that she place it in the church that she would establish at the location of Calvary. Helena had previously seen the Savior's Cross that Constantine had retained for himself, and she was aware that five more of the crosses were given by Constantine to the church, but she was still overwhelmed by the gift from the Pope of one of these magnificent golden anchor crosses. She had assured the Pope that she would, with the Lord's divine guidance, do everything in her power to make sure the gift was properly placed in the new church to be established at Calvary.

The Savior's Crosses were about 4 inches wide, 6 inches long, and one half inch thick. Each had a hole in the center of the vertical cross member toward the top of the cross that permitted it to be worn as a necklace by placing a length of leather cord or jeweled chain through the hole and then around the neck. Inscribed on the horizontal member of each cross were the Latin words **Pax Tecum**, meaning "Peace be with you". Most appropriate, since our Lord Jesus Christ once was, is now, and will forever be the Prince of Peace. Helena had placed her anchor cross on a necklace chain about her neck as soon as she returned from her visit with the Pope, and she now held the golden anchor cross in her hand and again marveled at its beauty and significance. Tears formed as she thought that the anchor cross she held was made from gold that had been blessed by the Lord.

Helena then retired for the evening, knowing she needed a good night's rest prior to the start of her long trip the following day. Her son Constantine would see her off the next morning, and she would be accompanied by a large contingency of servants and Roman soldiers. Sleep came quickly to Helena.

•••

The trip was long and taxing, over land and sea. But after many weeks Helena arrived in Jerusalem. Upon arrival she made contact with Bishop Macarius of Jerusalem. The Bishop arranged for suitable quarters for Helena and her entourage, and assisted in her quest to locate the true cross. After several weeks of searching, an excavation revealed three crosses. Helena was very hopeful that one of these was indeed the cross upon which Jesus Christ was crucified. But she required solid proof. After reflection, she had a woman near death brought to the site of the crosses. The woman was told to touch each of the crosses. After touching the first and then the second cross there was no discernable change in her condition. But when she touched the third cross she suddenly was immediately healed and released from her disease. Helena then proclaimed that cross to be the true cross, the one upon which the Lord was crucified. On the site where the cross was found Helena would have built the Church of the Holy Sepulchre. She later visited the sites of Jesus' birth at Bethlehem and of his ascension at the Mount of Olives, and on these sites she ordered the building of the Church of the Nativity and the Basilica of Olives, respectively.

Helena was most satisfied with locating the true cross. With the aid of Bishop Macarius she enlisted the assistance of the most accomplished wood craftsman in Jerusalem to remove pieces of wood from the cross to be taken back to Rome on her return journey. Many of these and other relics from her trip would be placed in her palace's private chapel in Rome. But before the long trip back to Rome, Helena had one very special task for the wood craftsman. She directed him to remove a section of wood from the cross and carve it into the exact shape of the anchor cross she wore about her neck. When finished, he was directed to join the wooden anchor cross to the back side of the Savior's Cross given to her by Pope Sylvester I. The wooden cross was to be the same thickness as the golden Savior's Cross. When completed, the anchor cross was transformed into one having two layers; the top layer was the original golden Savior's Cross as formed by Constantine, and the back layer was of wood from the true cross. Before leaving to return to Rome, Helena met with Bishop Macarius and presented him with the laminated anchor cross. The Bishop was stunned by its beauty, and tears formed in his eyes as Helena related the history of the Savior's cross. He then had to be seated when Helena told him that she was leaving the anchor cross with him to be permanently displayed in the Church of the Holy Sepulchre. Bishop Macarius expressed his deepest appreciation to Helena for her gift, and then proclaimed that it would henceforth be called The Helena Anchor Cross. The two embraced, and the following day Helena and her entourage started the long journey back to Rome. The year was 327 A.D.

Helena was very tired during the return trip. Because of her age she knew this would be her last journey. As she traveled toward Rome there was not a day that she did not think about the Helena Anchor Cross. She was satisfied that Bishop Macarius would care and protect the Anchor Cross with his life, and that it would be very inspirational to all those who would view it in the Church of the Holy Sepulchre. She did miss very much wearing the anchor cross. She reflected on the two occasions during the trip to Jerusalem when her life had been in great jeopardy, but on each occasion she was saved by an unexplainable and mysterious event. The first of these happened during the sea voyage across the Mediterranean Sea. The ship had encountered a vicious storm, and the captain had ordered all to abandon ship. Just as he had done so the sea suddenly calmed. Helena felt her chest becoming very warm, and when she felt the Savior's Cross being worn about her neck it felt hot. The second event happened on the land journey through Palestine to Jerusalem. Her entourage was going through a very narrow passage on a high hill when one wheel on her carpentum broke and the large 4-wheeled coach started to fall off a high cliff. But before it toppled over a mysterious and unexplainable force seemed to hold it in place until several of the Roman soldiers grabbed it on the side of the broken wheel and held it to allow Helena to step out. As she did so she again noticed her chest feeling very warm, and when she felt the Anchor Cross it again felt hot. Helena was convinced that on both of these occasions wearing the Anchor Cross somehow provided her with divine interventions that saved her life.

Helena was completely exhausted by the time she finally arrived back in Rome. Her health faded quickly after her trip, and she went to be with her Lord a short time later. Her son, Constantine the Great, continued as Roman Emperor until his death in 337 A.D. From the reports his mother had given him about her trip, Constantine monitored the building of the requested churches at the holy sites in Palestine.

Chapter 2

Harlan, Kentucky

Present time

Raymond Bell is pastor of the New Hope Baptist Church in Harlan. He sat at his desk in his church office. His secretary, Bonnie, had just brought in the morning mail and given it to him, and she returned to her office.

He spotted it immediately in the stack of mail. It was a large envelope from the office of the Archbishop of Washington, D.C. Several months ago Pastor Bell attended a conference in Washington that addressed opportunities for Christian ministry throughout the world. One that appealed greatly to Raymond was an ecumenical effort organized by the

Catholic church to minister to peoples of the archipelago of the Republic of Seychelles in the Indian Ocean. After hearing the presentation describing the need and opportunity to spread the word of Christ there, he accepted an application packet that was given to all ministers wishing to apply for the two week mission trip. Only twelve ministers would be selected, and those would be required to pay their own airfare. The Catholic Church would make arrangements for lodging, meals, and local transportation. Because he felt called to apply, Raymond had discussed this with his congregation, and they unanimously voted to pay for his airfare should he be selected, and they encouraged him to apply. Raymond felt sure that the envelope he now held in his hand was the response to his application. He first said a prayer, and then slowly started to open the envelope.

Bonnie was back at her desk drinking a cup of coffee when she heard a wall-splitting scream and she felt the floor shake from something going on in Pastor Bell's office. After spilling her coffee she stood and ran into his office. She found him holding a letter, with a giant grin on his face, and stomping up and down on the floor with his feet. He looked like her 8 year old son when he got his first bicycle for Christmas.

"Pastor Bell, are you okay?" Bonnie asked.

"Never felt better," Raymond replied. "This letter I just received says that I was accepted for the ecumenical mission trip to the Seychelles. There were hundreds that applied for the trip, and I was one of only twelve accepted. Praise the Lord!"

Raymond had been pastor at New Hope for about 14 years now. He was born and raised in Tavares, Florida. After finishing his Master's Degree in history at Florida State University, he married his childhood sweetheart, Betty, and they moved to Lexington, Kentucky where Raymond taught history and Betty taught art at Bryan Station High School. After a year Raymond felt called to the ministry, and enrolled at nearby Asbury Theological Seminary in Wilmore, Kentucky. Three years later he received a Master of Theology Degree, and then received a call from New Hope to become their new pastor. He accepted the call, and he and Betty moved to Harlan. They were warmly embraced by the congregation at New Hope, and also by all the people of Harlan. The last fourteen years in Harlan had been happy and productive for the couple.

Harlan is a small town in the mountains of Southeastern Kentucky. The population of the town has been dropping steadily, and currently has only about 1,500 residents. In fact, the population of all of Harlan County has declined steadily since the 1940 census put the county's population at 75,275. The 2010 census recorded only 29,278 in the county. The primary reason for the exodus is the decreasing number of jobs in the coal industry. In addition to the decreasing demand for coal, automation has replaced many of the jobs. And other than coal, Harlan County has little industry. The current largest source of revenue in the county is government checks. About a year ago there was the start of possibly a new revenue stream in the county when an Italian wine company, the Pelle Company of Prato, Italy, announced that it would develop a 100 acre section of Harlan County into a vineyard producing grapes of very high quality for the production of their quality wines. But monies from these and other vineyards now being cultivated in the county were still several years away.

Bonnie said, "Pastor, that's great news! Congratulations!!"

"Why thank you Bonnie," replied Pastor Bell. "I really had no idea I would be selected. I give thanks to the Lord."

"How soon will you be leaving?" she asked.

"The participants have several meetings to attend in preparation, and then we will all meet up in the capital city of Victoria, on Mahe island in the Seychelles during the first weekend of August. So the trip is still about three months away. Lots of preparation to do prior to going," said Raymond.

Bonnie replied, "Sure sounds exciting. You need to share the news with both the congregation and the people of Harlan. You can discuss the trip with the congregation at church services, but I think you should also contact the **Harlan Daily Enterprise** and get them to carry a story in the paper. News like this doesn't come along very frequently in Harlan!"

"Good idea, Bonnie," the pastor replied. "And I can't wait to get home to share the news with Betty. We discussed what she would do if I got lucky enough to go on the trip. She said she wanted to go to Florida to visit with her family while I'm gone, so she'll start those plans."

"Well, I'll leave you alone to think further about the trip. Let me know about any arrangements you would like me to make," said Bonnie.

"Sure will," replied Raymond. "Thanks!"

Chapter 3

Lexington, Kentucky

Dr. Randy Peters is Director of the University of Kentucky's Center for Appalachian Research (CAR), located in Lexington, Kentucky on the University's main campus. Randy has been the Center's Director for about twenty-one years. He received his undergraduate degree in sociology from the University of Kentucky and then Masters and Doctorate degrees in anthropology from the University of Virginia. His prime area of interest is the history and development of the Appalachian area. He had served five years on the anthropology faculty at UK prior to becoming the first and only Director of the CAR.

While Raymond and Betty Bell were living in Lexington they became good friends with Randy. They first met when Raymond and Betty decided to attend a seminar given by Randy addressing the history and development of Harlan County. After Randy's presentation they had several questions, and the three of them were in discussion for about a half hour. This led to Randy being invited to the Bell house for dinner, and their friendship continued to develop. It was Randy's expertise and interest in Harlan County that lead Raymond to apply for the pastor's position at Harlan's New Hope Baptist Church. And after Raymond and Betty moved to Harlan, they frequently talked and visited with Randy. It was a strong friendship.

The CAR had become world famous recently because it housed two artifacts that dated back to the time of Christ. Two of Constantine the Great's beautiful golden anchor crosses were on display in the CAR. Each of them were involved in events in Harlan County that were responsible for their finally being located in the CAR.

About thirteen years ago a ten-year-old boy, Kylie Potter, was hiking in a remote area of woods not far from Wallins, Kentucky, a community in Harlan County about 10 miles South of the city of Harlan. He stumbled upon some ruins from an early Harlan County settler, and in those ruins found what has become known as the Seibert Anchor Cross. Pastor Raymond Bell had called his friend Dr. Randy Peters to help in the investigation of the artifact, and it was through Randy's research that he traced the golden anchor cross back to Harlan pioneer Karl Seibert, and then back to its origin in Rome as one of Constantine's Savior's Crosses. The Seibert Anchor Cross was being worn by Kylie Potter while he was visiting with his mother, Carolyn, who was a teller at Harlan's Miners Bank. There was an attempted bank robbery which was aborted due to very unusual circumstances, later attributed to divine intervention somehow associated with the Seibert Anchor Cross. During this failed robbery, two safe deposit boxes containing about 3.5 million dollars in cash were opened. These monies were thought to be from the illegal drug trade, and were confiscated by the police. A distribution was made as follows, [1] 1.5 million dollars to Kylie Potter placed in a trust with his mother as the trustee, [2] one million dollars for construction of the Seibert Anchor Cross memorial on the grounds of the Harlan County Court House, and [3] one million dollars to the University of Kentucky's Center for Appalachian Research to both display the Seibert Anchor Cross and to be used for associated research. Kylie Potter retained ownership of the cross, but wanted it permanently placed in the CAR for study and viewing.

The second event involving a Savior's Cross occured only about seven months ago, on October 10th last year. A huge ceremony was held on the grounds of the Harlan County Court House. A part of the ceremony involved Dr. Randy Peters displaying another of the Savior's Crosses, called the Pelle Anchor Cross. One of Randy's colleagues discovered the cross in a church in Prato, Italy, and Randy had traveled there to see it and discovered it was owned by a Mr. Domenico Pelle. The very wealthy Mr. Pelle was owner of the extensive Pelle vineyards and winery. After quickly becoming friends, Randy and Dom Pelle traveled together to bring the Pelle Anchor Cross to the CAR for testing and analysis to verify it as one of the Savior's Crosses. During the October 10th ceremony a suicide bomber attempted to explode a bomb that would have killed hundreds, including one of Kentucky's U.S. Senators, but failed due to the presence of the Pelle Anchor Cross with it's mysterious power of divine intervention. Dom Pelle then decided to leave his anchor cross at the CAR permanently for viewing and research.

Over the past seven months the presence of the two Savior's Crosses in the CAR had generated tremendous world wide publicity. Historians, theologians, media, and great hordes of the general public had visited the CAR to view and have questions answered about the Seibert and Pelle Anchor Crosses. Dr. Randy Peters was a very busy man these days!

Chapter 4

Harlan, Kentucky

Fred Knapp, age 71, is mayor of the town of Harlan, a position he had held now for about eight years. He is very well liked and popular with most all that know him. Fred also owns and operates Creech Cafe, located directly across Central Street from the Harlan County Court house in downtown Harlan. He started working at Creech's, then owned by his father, immediately upon graduating from Harlan High School. That was fifty-three years ago. Creech cafe is a landmark in Harlan. It's a favorite hang-out for kids, stopping in daily after school to have a snack and swap stories with their classmates. Lots of old timers also spend time daily at Creech's, discussing the current news and solving all the world's problems. Two distinctive features immediately present themselves to anyone walking into Creech Cafe. The first is a greeting from Polly. About twenty-three years old now, Polly is a large, green parrot that perches on a rod mounted above and to the side of the front door. "Polly want a cracker, Polly want a cracker," she will usually squawk at those entering. Most ignore her, but some will speak to her, and some will even stroke her feathers. She loves to beg food from the customers, and often times is successful. The second unique feature at Creech's is that all the walls are plastered with photographs and written articles related in some way to the town of Harlan. There are thousands of these. Fred selects which are worthy to go on his walls, and once posted they seldom come down. Fred knows the stories behind each posting, and loves to share these with interested customers. He's been known to spend hours telling customers everything associated with a given posting.

Pastor Bell just entered Creech's.

"Morning Preach, Morning Preach," Polly squawked.

Pastor Bell reached up and gave the bird a gentle pet and said, "Your eyesight is still good Polly, it is I." He then walked in and sat down at a table toward the front of the cafe. Creech's had about twenty stools along the counter, a dozen booths, and twenty-four tables. The cash register was on the counter beside the entrance door.

"Top of the morning Pastor Bell," said a cheery Fred Knapp as he approached Raymond's table with a carafe of coffee.

"And a big ole good morning to you as well my friend," Raymond replied. "That coffee smells super, as usual!"

Fred poured Raymond's cup full, and then sat down at the table with him, placing the carafe toward the back of the table. "What's up with you this fine morning," Fred asked.

"Well, a lot actually," Raymond replied. "And I wanted to share some news with you."

At that moment Harlan County Sheriff J. Bert Sterling and his chief deputy, Kyle Potter, walked in the front door.

"Head for the hills, head for the hills, the law's here," Polly squawked.

Deputy Potter reached up and stroked Polly, and then the two walked to the table and sat with Fred and Raymond.

"Hope you don't mind the law joining you guys for coffee," Sheriff Sterling asked.

"Welcome, welcome," Fred said, as he and Raymond shook hands with Bert and Kyle.

"Pastor Bell here was just getting ready to share some news with me," Fred said. "Okay if the law hears it too?"

"Yes indeed," Raymond replied. "As a matter of fact, I want everyone in Harlan County to know this news!"

"We're all ears," Kyle replied.

"Well, several months ago you may recall that I attended a meeting in Washington that addressed opportunities for world-wide ministry. There was one ecumenical trip to minister to folks in Seychelles that caught my interest, and I wound up applying for it." Raymond said.

"I recall your discussing that in church a while back," Bert replied. Fred and Kyle nodded in agreement, since they all attended New Hope Baptist.

"Well, yesterday I got a response," replied Raymond.

"Let me guess," said Fred. "I think I see a long trip in store for you!"

"Indeed," replied Raymond, and he went on to tell them all about the letter.

"That really is big and exciting news, Raymond," responded Kyle. "I assume you will be sharing the news with your congregation and with the **_Harlan Daily Enterprise_**."

"Yes, I just dropped off a description of the upcoming trip with the ***Enterprise*** on my way over here. They seemed very pleased, and said they would write it up as a feature story in the week-end edition." Raymond said.

"Do you know any of the others that were selected? And exactly how will you go about doing the ministry there?" Fred asked.

"Those are excellent questions!" Raymond responded. "As I had told you, there were a total of only twelve selected. Six of these are Catholic priests and 6 are protestant. There was one other Baptist, two Methodists, and two Presbyterians selected. My understanding is that a Catholic priest and a protestant will form six different teams. By far the most predominant religion of the Seychelles is Catholicism. So that's the reason for having a Catholic priest on each team. Most everyone there does speak English, so communication should not pose a problem. The Catholic Church will arrange a schedule that will take each two-member team to visit in a number of the 116 islands that make up the archipelago. Obviously, we will concentrate on those with significant population. There are only a total of about 90,000 souls living there. The largest island is Mahe, where their capital city of Victoria is located. The Catholic church will arrange all the transportation and housing. We will have to do some trips by water, and some by air. During our two week visit each team will visit five different sites. At each one we will visit with people at the local establishments during the day and conduct a 2 hour long service each evening. It will be a very busy two weeks, but I'm looking forward greatly to it. What a challenge!"

Kyle asked, "I really hate to sound so dumb, but exactly where are the Seychelles?" Fred and Bert grinned and nodded in agreement.

"Oh, I'm sorry Kyle. I should have told you that at the beginning. And that's not a dumb question at all. They really are not well known by any means," the Pastor replied. "The Republic of Seychelles, pronounced 'say-shelz' . . . it's French, is located almost 1,000 miles east of mainland Southeast Africa. A little better known and much larger island, Madagascar, is located Southwest of the Seychelles."

"Thanks," Kyle said. "Now I have in my mind where it's located."

There was a sudden rush of wind as Polly sailed just over their heads on the way to mooch food from a customer sitting at a table toward the back of the cafe. The customer had only to hold up a nibble of food between two fingers and call "Polly" and she would immediately answer the call for food.

Raymond said, "Well, we've had our coffee and I've bent your ears too long with my upcoming trip, so I guess we need to all get back to work."

"Everyone except Fred, Pastor, he's already at work!" replied the Sheriff.

Fred chuckled and said, "Gents, the coffee's on the house . . . you all have a good day!"

After thanking Fred, the three left Creech's. Raymond departed for the church, and Bert and Kyle headed across the street to the Sheriff's office, which is in a building immediately adjacent to the Court House. It consists essentially of four large rooms. Upon entering there is a reception area and desks for two deputies. Walking on through the reception area the next room is that for the Sheriff, and further back there are two additional rooms. One is a small cell capable of holding maybe up to 6 prisoners, and the other is an evidence storage room. The storage room has a rear door exiting the building.

Bert and Kyle walked in the front door of the Sheriff's office. Deputy Rosie Cain greeted the two of them, "Hi guys, was the coffee and conversation good at Creech's?"

Bert replied, "Excellent on both counts, as always."

Bert continued to his office, and Deputy Kyle informed Rosie about the conversation with Pastor Bell discussing his upcoming trip.

Rosie said, "Gee, that will be some trip!! Half-way around the world. And close to Africa, home to all those great wild animals!"

Rosie was a true animal lover. She and her husband had two dogs and several cats. In addition, she was caretaker for Preacher Puss, the resident cat at the Sheriff's office. Preacher Puss had gotten his name when he was discovered by fireman fighting a fire at a church in Harlan County about 13 years ago. The cat, a 15 pound gray tabby, was found screaming at the top of her lungs in a smoke filled storage room in the back of the church. The fireman rescued her and took her to a vet to be checked out. They then returned her to the pastor at the church, but he informed them that he had never seen the cat before, and that it must have just wondered into the church storage room when the door was left open. So the fireman took the cat to the sheriff's office, where Rosie fell in love with her and made comfortable arrangements for her to live there. Although Bert objected at first, he soon relented and he and all the other deputies had soon adopted Preacher Puss as their own. Rosie gave her the name because she was found screaming in a church. She loved to look out the window of the Sheriff's office, so one of the deputies made her a shelf above and to the side of the front door. She would spend most of her time laying on this shelf looking out the window, swishing her tail and gently purring. To reach this shelf she would jump from the floor to the deputy's desk and then on up to the shelf.

Preacher Puss had truly become a legend in the Sheriff's office. On several occasions now she had even been responsible for catching criminals. Unlike any other cat anyone had heard of, Preacher Puss had a special peculiarity. She hated guns! This was first discovered soon after she came to the Sheriff's office. A deputy drew his pistol and was ready to start cleaning it when Preacher Puss leaped from her shelf onto the deputy's arm holding the pistol. She dug into the arm with her claws and started screaming. He dropped the gun, and she immediately pulled back her claws and climbed back to her shelf. And then on several other occasions criminals had come into the sheriff's office with gun in hand only to have Preacher Puss leap from her shelf, screaming, to the top of their heads and dig in her claws. They always dropped their guns! Preacher Puss quickly became well known and respected in the law enforcement community around Harlan County. Those that knew her always reached up to her shelf as they entered and gave her several affectionate strokes, and she would always reply with a big meow and a rapidly swishing tail.

J. Bert Sterling, sixty-one-years-old, has been sheriff of Harlan County for the past twenty-seven years. He joined as a deputy upon graduation from Harlan High School, and after 15 years ran for sheriff and was overwhelmingly elected. He has remained extremely popular, and has never been seriously challenged in an election. Bert is tall, thin, and most say very handsome. He has devoted his entire life to law enforcement. He has never married, but sees Carolyn Potter frequently.

Deputy Kyle Potter, son of Carolyn, joined the sheriff's department only about a year ago upon his graduation from Eastern Kentucky University's Law Enforcement Program. The events of thirteen years ago, when Kyle, then called Kylie, found the Seibert Anchor Cross resulted in his having a 1.5 million dollar trust fund established which enabled him to pursue his college education and still have a very nice balance remaining. Kyle is a very dedicated deputy, and sheriff Sterling recognized this and appointed him as chief deputy. His desk in the sheriff's office is in the reception area, along with that of Deputy Rosie Cain. It was Kyle's desk that Preacher Puss jumped to on her way to and from her shelf.

Deputy Rosie Cain served mainly as a clerk for the sheriff's department, but occasionally was called upon for other duties.

Because of it's limited budget, due largely to the continually decreasing tax base, the sheriff's office was only open sixteen hours per day (two shifts), Monday through Saturday, and only eight hours on Sunday. In addition to the main office in Harlan there was a satellite office in Cumberland, about twenty-five miles Northeast of Harlan on Route 119. Each office has a total of five deputies. In addition to Rosie Cain and Kyle Potter there was deputy Simpson Brown on the first shift. Simpson normally was on patrol in a cruiser. The second shift in Harlan was deputies Mousy Giles and Bill Black. Mousy usually worked in the office, and Bill patrolled in a cruiser. The Cumberland office had similar shifts. Calls that came to the sheriff's office when it was closed were redirected to the Kentucky State Police post 10, located just outside Harlan on Highway 421.

Chapter 5

Faure Plantation, Mahe Island, Seychelles

1860

In 1770 the French settled the Seychelles. Large plantations were set up which produced cotton, rice, sugar, and maize. These plantations relied heavily on slave labor, but were changed after the Napoleonic Wars when the British took control. In 1835 the British prohibited slavery.

Jean-Paul Faure had established a large plantation on the Northeastern shore of Mahe Island. The plantation produced a variety of crops, and after about 40 years of development it was one of the largest and most profitable plantations in the

Seychelles. Jean-Paul Faure was a very wealthy man. Unlike a lot of the plantation owners, he was also a very good man. He treated his workers fairly, and paid them wages that exceeded most in the area. He was also a Christian, and about five years ago had asked the Catholic church to establish a small chapel on his plantation where he and his workers could worship. The Catholic and Anglican churches had opened mission schools in 1851, and Faure had asked that an Anglican mission school be located on his plantation to teach the children of his workers. Both requests were granted.

Jean-Paul enjoyed greatly riding horses around his plantation. It was late in the afternoon of a beautiful October day when he found himself riding along the seashore. He had been attracted to the shore when he noticed a lot of flotsam scattered along the water's edge. He galloped at a slow gait as he inspected what appeared to be everything from pieces of wood, both small and large, to articles of clothing, pieces of paper, and other unidentifiable items. He concluded that a ship must have sunk, likely after striking one of the numerous coral reefs North of Mahe.

He then glanced out to sea and saw a chilling sight. What appeared to be two men were huddled atop a large piece of wood, floating toward shore. Jean-Paul got off his horse and started walking toward the shore where the men would make land. He then saw that they were using their hands to paddle toward shore. They soon got close to shore and jumped off their raft. Once out of the water they collapsed onto the sand beach.

Upon reaching them Jean-Paul said, "Are you able to speak?"

Each man looked to be only about eighteen-years-old. One had red hair, and he answered with a shaky, hardly audible voice, "Yes, just barely. We have been adrift for three days. The ship we were on sank."

The other young man, with dark black hair, did not speak.

"In just a moment I'll ride and get you food and water," replied Jean-Paul. "But I would like to know what ship you were on and whether you know if there might be other survivors."

Red hair replied, "The ship was the *Aqaba Maiden,* and we did not see any others. There was a terrible storm that forced the ship onto coral banks. It was night, and at daybreak we saw no other survivors. And then we just drifted for three days."

Jean-Paul then asked, "How many were on the ship?"

Red hair responded, "Thirty."

Jean-Paul then said, "Rest here, and I'll be back shortly with help for you"

As he was turning to retrieve his horse Jean-Paul noticed Red hair appearing to hold something under his water drenched shirt. He had his right hand over something hung about his neck and under his shirt.

Jean-Paul asked Red hair, "What's that under your shirt?"

Red hair replied, "Nothing. Just a good luck piece. For some reason it feels very warm . . . probably my imagination."

Jean-Paul nodded, mounted his horse, and rode off.

• • •

After getting back to his plantation home, Jean-Paul directed his foreman to take a couple of workers and horses and retrieve the two drifters. The foreman was told to take them to the worker's building, provide them fresh clothes, feed them and bunk them for the night. He was directed to bring them to the plantation home the next morning after breakfast.

Jean-Paul lived with his wife Caroline and three sons in the grand and spacious plantation home. They had a full complement of servants.

At 9 am a servant answered the knock on the door, and after greeting the foreman brought the two drifters to meet with Jean-Paul in his study.

The servant announced the two gentleman to Jean-Paul. The study was large and very elaborately decorated. Shelves containing books filled one wall, and comfortable furniture was located in front of Jean-Paul's desk.

Jean-Paul motioned for the two to have a seat on a sofa directly in front of his desk. He rose and came around the desk and shook hands with each drifter, and then returned to be seated behind his desk.

"First, I think we should do names," Jean-Paul said. "My name is Jean-Paul Faure, and the property you are now on is known as the Faure Plantation. I have been the owner of this plantation since it was formed some forty years ago."

After a brief pause, Red hair said, "Thank you Mr. Faure. People just call me Red".

Black hair then said, "I'm called Bones."

"Red, Bones, I'm pleased to meet you. I trust you were well fed and had a good night's rest," Jean-Paul said.

Red responded, "We sure did. We were just about dead. We are very, very grateful for all your help, Mr. Faure." Bones nodded in agreement.

"Perhaps you could tell me a bit more about your ship, I think you said it was called the *Aqaba Maiden,* where you came from and where you were going," asked Jean-Paul.

Red looked at Bones, and then said, "Well, the ship left Jordan from the port of Aqaba. We sailed down the Sea of Aqaba to the Red Sea and then South into the Indian Ocean. After about two weeks we encountered the huge storm. Our ship was only about 100-feet-long, and the storm quickly drove us onto a reef. The bottom started taking on water, and in a short time the Captain said we were going down. We had two small boats, but they quickly filled and left the ship. Many of the crew just grabbed something to float on and jumped overboard. I could not swim, so I stayed on the ship until the stern filled with water and the bow raised up out of the water at a steep angle. When that happened I slid to the very back of the ship, along with a lot of cargo boxes. The boxes began to break up as they slammed into the stern. Bones came flying back and almost hit me as he stopped at the rail. We both saw a large piece of wood that had broken off a crate and grabbed it and jumped into the water. It was night, and dark. We didn't see anything until daybreak, and then all we saw was small pieces of wood and other stuff from the ship floating around. We saw no people."

Jean-Paul asked, "Where was the ship headed and what was its cargo?"

Red replied, "Bones and me were just crew. They didn't tell us anything. At the Port of Aqaba we got hired on . . . we're both just from very poor families and were looking for any kind of work. We both had experience on fishing ships, so they hired us. Along the way we sort-of got the idea from listening to other crew and occasionally from the leaders that we were carrying some kind of loot that had been stolen and they were taking it to a port called Durban in South Africa where they had contacts that were going to buy it. That's about all we knew about it."

"I see," Jean-Paul said. He looked at Bones and said, "Does that sound right to you Bones?"

Bones spoke, "It does. We don't know no more than that. We just lucky to be alive. We sure thank you for your help Mr. Faure."

Jean-Paul continued, "Okay, I know you're tired. But you both look like very strong and able bodied men. If you would like, I would hire you to work on the plantation. I'm always in need of good workers. You would be well paid and expected to work hard and to behave yourselves. What'd you say?"

Red answered, "It's like a dream! Yesterday we were drifting on the ocean with little hope of staying alive, and today we are not only alive, but offered jobs! You bet, Mr. Faure. We'll work very hard for you and we'll certainly behave ourselves. We'll try and be the best workers on the plantation. You'll just have to show us what to do."

Bones chimed in, "Red said it all. Thanks so much Mr. Faure!"

"Okay, boys, my Foreman will take you back to your quarters and get you started. We'll talk more later. Welcome to the Faure Plantation," replied Jean-Paul.

• • •

Ten months later

The maid answered the knock on the Plantation House door, and welcomed Red. She then took him to the study where Jean-Paul was waiting for him. Red had requested a meeting the previous day.

"Welcome, welcome Red," Jean-Paul greeted. "Please have a seat and tell me what you wish to talk about."

Red said, "Thanks Mr. Faure. I had a little matter I wanted to discuss with you. Me and Bones have been really happy here at the plantation. It's been the best thing that ever happened to us. We feel like family. We've taken advantage of the school, and also of the chapel. Me and Bones are now Christians. We really cannot thank you enough Mr. Faure. We've even been able to save a lot of our wages, and hopefully before too long we'll be able to buy a small place somewhere off the plantation to live, but still will work for you, of course."

"That sounds really good, Red," Jean-Paul replied. "I've been really pleased with the job you and Bones have done for me, and you're welcome to work here as long as you wish."

"Thanks, Mr. Faure," Red replied. "There's something else I want to discuss with you. Do you remember when you found us you asked me what I was holding under my shirt?"

"I do," said Jean-Paul. "And I think you said it was a good luck charm, or something like that."

"That's right," Red said. "And I didn't lie about that. It certainly brought us good luck on that raft. But I think it might be more than a good luck charm." Then Red reached behind his neck and grabbed the necklace and pulled it over his head. Out from under his shirt appeared a beautiful wooden anchor cross. Red held the anchor cross in his right hand.

Jean-Paul's eyes got very large, and he said, "Red, that is gorgeous! I have never seen a more beautiful anchor cross."

And then Red reached down with his left hand and gently turned the anchor cross over. It's golden brilliance was astounding.

Jean-Paul stood from his seat and walked around his desk. His eyes were wide and he had a look on his face that radiated his surprise.

"I have never, never, seen anything like that," he said. "This side appears to be pure gold, and the craftsmanship of it and of the wooden anchor cross are beyond my understanding. Where did you get this?"

"Do you remember my telling you about the storm and how the wooden cargo boxes slid down into the stern of the ship and broke open?" asked Red.

"I do," replied Jean-Paul.

"Well, when one of them cracked open a lot of beautiful jewels, vases, and other valuable things spilled out. This anchor cross was one of them. It was the only thing I had time to grab before abandoning ship onto the raft. It had the necklace attached, so I just put it around my neck and under my shirt. Not even Bones knew about it. The whole time we were adrift I kept having this strange feeling that everything would turn out okay. It's hard to describe. It was just a feeling like something was directing us and that we shouldn't worry. And then when we finally made land and you found us, the anchor-cross seemed to be hot, and my chest felt very warm. It was really a strange sensation. I don't understand it, but after me and Bones became Christians after attending many church services in the plantation chapel, I then seemed to get the feeling that somehow the anchor cross must have provided us with divine guidance. After all, the cross is the symbol for Christianity. It does represent the cross on which Jesus died for our sins. What do you think Mr. Faure?"

Jean-Paul ran his fingers over the golden anchor cross. He then gently lifted it, turned it over, and ran his fingers over the beautiful wooden anchor cross. He then said, "Red, never have I seen anything like this. I just don't know what to think. Do you have any idea where this came from?"

Red replied, "I really don't. The stories that we heard on the ship were that the leaders and several of the crew had just come from a trip into Palestine in which they robbed many places of valuable things. This must be one of those."

"Amazing," said Jean-Paul.

"Mr. Faure, I know this anchor cross is stolen. And I know it is very valuable. But we don't know where it came from. What I would like to do is to donate it to the chapel to be displayed. I think it might inspire nonbelievers to think about the meaning of the cross, and hopefully to becoming Christians. Would that be okay with you?"

"Red, it would be more than okay with me," replied Jean-Paul. "I will arrange for it to be placed in the chapel. I will make sure it is secure. Thank you so much. I feel certain that it will inspire many that view it to understand the true meaning of the cross."

Chapter 6

Harlan County, Kentucky

Present time

Maggard's Grocery is located on highway 119 about 10 miles South of the town of Harlan, and about 1 mile from the community of Wallins. It is a very small, country grocery and only averages a few customers each day.

"Good morning Mrs. Johnson," Fatso Chapel said. "I trust you found everything you were looking for."

Fatso was the only clerk in the grocery store. He usually could be found seated behind the counter at the check-out either watching a small television or reading novels. There was no cash register, just a cash box located in a shelf under the counter. He used an old adding machine with a paper print out roll to tally the groceries.

"Yes, Fatso, I think I found everything. I only needed a few things this morning," replied Mrs. Johnson.

"That'll be $12.75 Mrs. Johnson," Fatso said.

Mrs. Johnson handed Fatso a ten and a five.

Fatso said, "Okay Mrs. Johnson, here's your change, $2.25. You have a good day . . . always good seeing you."

Mrs. Johnson placed the change in her purse, and started to lift the two small bags of groceries, and said, "Thank you Fatso, always good to see you. I hope your day is good as well!"

Fatso then replied, "Mrs. Johnson, do you know why elephants seldom go to college?"

Mrs. Johnson got a grin on her face and slowly shook her head.

"Because very few elephants finish High School!" Fatso said with a giggle.

Mrs. Johnson was still shaking her head as she went out the door.

Fatso just loved to tell corny jokes. All the local customers that came into Maggard's were always prepared to listen to one. Any strangers that happened in usually did not know what to think of his humor. But he kept telling them anyway.

Maggard's grocery was just a front for a lot of illegal activity that originated in the room in the back of the store. At the rear of the grocery was a door that could only be opened when Fatso pressed a button under the check-out counter that unlocked the door. Inside the back room was the office of Trigger Green. Trigger had owned the grocery now for about thirteen years. He acquired it after the previous owner, Pretty Boy Maggard, got in a bunch of trouble when, during a botched bank robbery, 3.5 million dollars of illegal drug money was uncovered in two lock boxes rented by Pretty Boy. Both Pretty Boy and Trigger fled the country to Columbia, South America. Pretty Boy stayed there, but Trigger got home sick and returned after about 6 months. Pretty Boy arranged to transfer title of Maggard's to Trigger. Sheriff Sterling had tried to tie some of the illegal drug money and activity to Trigger, but couldn't since everything was in Pretty Boy's name. Pretty Boy was involved in a lot of different illegal activities, but his main income came from laundering drug money for various Eastern Kentucky drug dealers. One of his main customers was Big Jim Owens from Prestonsburg, Kentucky. When Pretty Boy left the country, Big Jim took over his money laundering business, so now Trigger was involved in any illegal activity that he thought he could get away with, including book-making, moonshine, credit card theft, car theft, various fraud schemes, etc. But to his credit, during the events of last October 10th he and Fatso had been responsible for saving the lives of hundreds when they prevented a suicide bomber from detonating a bomb at a large ceremony being held at the Harlan County Court House. Sheriff Sterling unraveled the puzzle and discovered that they were somehow involved in the scheme, but that they had decided not be a part of murdering hundreds of people and had prevented it from happening. Bert had finally talked to Pretty Boy and Fatso about this, and they acknowledged "off the record" their part, but since the sheriff had no evidence against them there were no charges. The sheriff just shook their hands and thanked them for saving hundreds of lives. No one knew the true story other than the three of them.

Trigger walked out of his office through the grocery store on his way to lunch.

He said, "Hey Fatso, hold down the store. I'm headed out for lunch."

Fatso responded, "Hey Trigger, you know how you put six elephants in a Volkswagen?"

Trigger just kept walking toward the door.

"You put three in the front seat and three in the back seat!" Fatso said with a giggle.

Trigger slammed the door on his way out.

Chapter 7

Harlan, Kentucky

Ole Bennie was the town drunk. He spent as much time in jail for being drunk as he did outside jail. All the deputies were well acquainted with Bennie, and he usually wasn't too much of a problem to arrest and get to jail. Today he was. Today Bennie wanted to fight. Simpson Brown had received the call about 2 pm. Bennie was just outside the Harlan Post Office asking everyone coming and going for a handout, and if he didn't get one he wanted to fight. When Deputy Brown arrived Bennie had a terrified elderly lady pinned up against the post office door. Several citizens were just watching. When Simpson got to Bennie and told him to release the lady and put his hands up, Bennie did release the lady but rather than putting his hands up he took a drunken swing at Deputy Brown, who really wasn't expecting it because normally Bennie is pretty docile. The swing caught Simpson on the nose, and it immediately started to bleed. He finally got Bennie cuffed and in his cruiser and off to jail.

Deputy Brown and Bennie walked into the Sheriff's Department. Simpson's face was covered in blood, so he immediately took off Bennie's handcuffs and sat him down at Deputy Potter's desk just inside the door. He then cuffed his left hand to a water pipe going up the wall beside the desk and said, "Bennie you sit there and behave for a minute till I can get cleaned up and I'll be back to put you in the lockup."

Rosie Cain was near hysterical when she saw all the blood on Simpson's face. She immediately ran into the Sheriff's office where the first aid kit was kept and told Simpson to follow her. She began to clean his face and apply first aid.

Meantime, Bennie, being the inquisitive person that he was, in addition to being drunk, used his free right hand to open Deputy Potter's desk drawers to see what he might be able to find. As soon as he opened the right hand drawer he saw a gun. It was a pearl-handle .38 revolver! He immediately grabbed the gun with his free right hand and held it out, waiting for the two deputies to come back into the reception room. Suddenly there was a very high-pitched scream, followed by a big thud on the top of his head, with long gray hair falling down on all sides, and then the worst pain Bennie had ever experienced. Blood started to pour down his face and a long, swishing gray tail spread the blood all over his face. Bennie dropped the gun and screamed at the top of his lungs, "Help, help, somebody help. A monster's got me!"

As Rosie and Simpson came running back into the reception room they saw Preacher Puss back on his shelf above Deputy Potter's desk, and Bennie sitting cuffed to his desk with his face completely covered in blood and the 38 revolver laying on the floor. Bennie's eyes were big as saucers, and his trembling voice said, "I'll never touch another drop as long as I live....just keep that monster away from me!"

Rosie and Simpson both could not contain a smile and chuckle. Rosie went back into the sheriff's office to get the first-aid kit for Bennie, and Simpson walked over to Bennie and uncuffed him from the water pipe.

"Maybe that'll teach you to lay off that booze and quit attacking an officer," Simpson said.

"Yes sir, I've learned my lesson. No more booze. No more fighting. From now on I'm a sober, peaceable man," Bennie said. He still had not seen Preacher Puss on his shelf, and had no idea who or what had attacked him. Rosie administered first aid, and Simpson, after placing the gun back in Kyle's desk, took Bennie to the lockup to sleep it off.

When Simpson got back to the reception room, he and Rosie burst out laughing aloud. Rosie reached up and handed Preacher Puss three or four *Whisker Lickin* cat treats. Simpson reached up and stroked Preacher Puss as she devoured the treats. The cat then curled up, got a very contented look on her face, started swishing her long tail, closed her eyes, and seemed to doze off with her 'motor' running." Just another days work for Preacher Puss. Another criminal captured.

• • •

With Deputy Simpson Brown back on his patrol duty, and Deputy Rosie Cain back to her normal routine, Sheriff J. Bert Sterling and Chief Deputy Kyle Potter walked in the front door of the sheriff's department. Rosie had to immediately tell them all about the Bennie-Preacher Puss encounter. They all laughed for a good long time.

"Well, chalk one more up for ole Preacher Puss, the least paid and one of the most efficient law enforcement members around these parts. I'll have to buy her something special.... maybe a pound of salmon," Bert said. Kyle reached up and stroked the cat. She bellowed a loud meow in approval.

Chapter 8

Harlan, Kentucky

Sheriff Sterling and Deputy Potter walked through the door at Creech Cafe. It was 3 pm in the afternoon, and they needed a coffee break.

"The law's here, the law's here, head for the hills, head for the hills," Polly squawked. Kyle reached up and stroked her feathers.

"That feels good. That feels good." She said.

"Behave yourself, Polly" Bert said to her as he and Kyle walked to a table and had a seat.

Mayor Knapp soon appeared, poured coffee, and then had a seat with them. He said, "You boys look like you need a little caffeine."

"Yeah, we sure do. Been hard at catching crooks all day. We need a bit of a break," Bert responded.

"Well, you came to the right place," Fred responded. "Can I get you anything to eat? How about a doughnut?"

"Not for me, thanks," Bert replied.

"No, I'm fine too," Kyle said.

"Well, at least I might be able to cheer you up a bit," Fred said. "See that newspaper article posted on the wall there beside you Kyle?"

Kyle and Bert looked at it. It appeared to be a rather lengthy story about the recently retired physician from Harlan's Daniel Boone Clinic, Dr. Clyde Costello. There was a large picture of Dr. Costello at the start of the article. Both nodded to Fred as they looked it over.

Fred began, "Well, that article was in last weekend's **Enterprise**. I know you boys are too busy to read the paper, so let me tell you the story. Dr. Costello retired at the age of 75 just about a week ago. The Daniel Boone Clinic held a big celebration party for him, and at one point during the evening he was asked what was the most embarrassing moment he had encountered during his long medical career. Dr. Costello though for a short moment, a big grin came on his face, and he said he was going to then tell a very embarrassing story, and he would tell it only because he was now retired and he and his wife now planned to move to Hawaii. The audience became very quiet and were all ears. Dr. Costello started by saying that he was born and raised in Chicago. He had lots of family still there. He received his Medical Degree from the University of Chicago, and then after an internship set up practice in Chicago, the city he loved. After about ten years he had achieved a world reputation as an expert in a certain medical area and the University of Chicago invited him to present a lecture on the subject at a large conference. When it was time for his presentation, he walked on stage and placed his papers on the lectern, but they slid off onto the floor. As he bent over to retrieve them he inadvertently passed gas … and very loudly! The excellent sound system microphone amplified the sound resoundingly throughout the room and it reverberated down the hall. Dr. Costello was very embarrassed, but somehow regained his composure enough to deliver his paper. At the conclusion, he ignored the applause and raced out the side door, never to be seen in his home town again, and started practicing medicine in Harlan. Decades later his elderly mother was ill and he returned to Chicago to visit her. He reserved a hotel room under the name of Smith and arrived under the cover of darkness. The desk clerk asked him, 'Is this your first visit to our city, Mr. Smith' Dr. Costello replied, 'Well, young man, no, it isn't. I grew up here and received my education here, but then I moved away'. 'Why haven't you visited?' asked the desk clerk. 'Actually I had a very embarrassing thing happen here and since then I've been too ashamed to return.' Dr. Costello replied. The clerk then said, 'Sir, while I don't have your life experience, one thing I have learned is that often what seems embarrassing to one isn't even remembered by others. I bet that's true in your case.' Dr. Costello replied, 'Son, I would like to think that was true in my case.' The clerk then asked, 'Was it a long time ago?' Dr. Costello said, 'Many years'. The clerk then asked, 'Was it before or after the famous Costello fart?' "

Bert, Kyle, and Fred started laughing so hard that all the other customers in Creech's turned to see what was going on.

Bert then said, "I can certainly see why Dr. Costello didn't tell that story until he was getting ready to leave town! I bet he and his wife were on the plane to Hawaii the next morning!"

Fred responded, "Likely."

Kyle then said, "Thanks Fred, that story made our day. After hearing that I think Bert and I will be able to catch several more crooks before the day's over!"

Just then Polly squawked, "Here's the preach, here's the preach, watch your language, watch your language."

Pastor Raymond Bell reached up and gave Polly a stroke, and then walked over to join Fred, Bert, and Kyle.

"Have a seat Pastor," said Bert. "You just missed one of Fred's best. About Dr. Costello" And Bert pointed to the article on the wall.

"Oh yes," replied Raymond. "Betty and I read that article in the **Enterprise**. We both laughed so hard we got stomach cramps."

"So, how's all the plans going for the big trip?" asked Fred.

"Going very well, thank you," replied Raymond. "I finally got my plane ticket. That's going to be some plane trip. I fly out of Lexington. My ticket is through KLM, the Royal Dutch Airlines. Delta is an affiliate, so I first fly from Lexington to Atlanta. I'm reminded of the old adage that when you die and go either up or down you'll first have to pass through Atlanta! Anyway, after getting to Atlanta I have about an hour layover and then fly to Amsterdam, and have an eleven-hour layover. Then to Abu Dhabi and a two hour layover. And then finally to Victoria, Seychelles. All together I have about twenty hours of time in the air, but about thirty-five hours from Lexington to Victoria. I'll need some recovery time after that flight!"

"Don't think I could do it at my age," replied Fred.

"So do you know any more about the specifics of your itinerary after you get to the Seychelles?" asked Bert.

Raymond responded, "Yeah, a bit more. As I told you previously, one catholic priest will be paired up with one protestant pastor, and there will be six such teams. Each team will visit 5 different sites during the two week period. I have been assigned to a Father Elmer Schmidt from Chicago."

Fred broke in and said, "Be sure to ask Father Schmidt if he has heard of the famous Costello fart!"

After another hearty round of laughing Raymond continued, "I received the itinerary for Father Schmidt and myself. We will be first visiting a large plantation on the Northeastern part of the Island of Mahe. Victoria is also on Mahe. We'll stay 2 days at this plantation and then move to a village in the very Southern part of the island, and after two days there we move to a small village just outside Victoria, still on

Mahe. We then board a boat and go to the island of Silhouette, located Northwest of Mahe. The last stop is on North Island, just north of Silhouette. We will then fly back to Victoria in a small plane arranged by the sponsoring catholic church. I then fly back home, another thirty-five-hour trip. You might need to reserve a room for me at the hospital upon my return . . . I'll be completely worn out!!"

"Ahh, but a very worthwhile and rewarding trip," said Fred. "I can't wait to hear the stories that you'll have."

Kyle asked, "At each of the stops, what exactly will you be doing?"

Raymond responded, "There is a coordinator at each site. The coordinator will take us around to meet and visit with local people and establishments, and to the local church where we will conduct a two hour service each night. Hopefully we will attract some that have not heard the Word previously, or at least not accepted it, and perhaps, with the Lord's guidance, some will make decisions to become Christians. That's the purpose of the trip, of course."

"And will the coordinator provide for your lodging and meals at each site?" asked Fred

"That's the plan," replied Raymond.

"Wow! What an exciting and rewarding trip, Raymond," said Bert.

"It should certainly be," responded Raymond. "And it's just about a month off now. I've got to start thinking about my clothes and other stuff I need to pack."

"Betty will help there, I'm sure," said Kyle.

"I'm sure she will, and she'll have her own packing to do to take her Florida trip while I'm gone," said Raymond.

"Speaking of working so hard that you might drop, reminded me of another story," Fred said. He then stood up and pointed to a picture posted on the wall of a man playing a bagpipe at an apparent gravesite.

Everyone looked at the picture, and Raymond said, "I don't recall hearing a story about that one, Fred."

"Well, you're getting ready to hear it now," Bert said as he and Kyle and Raymond got big grins on their faces.

Fred began, "Well, as you can see by the picture, the guy plays the bagpipes. He lives in Cumberland, and is asked to play at all kinds of different events. Recently he was asked by a funeral director in Cumberland if he would play at a graveside service for a homeless man. The deceased had no family or friends, so the service was to be at a pauper's cemetery in a remote area about 5 miles from Cumberland. The bagpiper felt very sorry for the homeless person, and agreed to play at his graveside. The funeral director then gave the bagpiper the directions to the grave site. The bagpiper had not been there before, and he got lost on his way. Being a man, he didn't stop for directions. He finally arrived at what he thought was the site about an hour late and saw that the funeral guy and hearse had already left. There were only the diggers and crew left and they were having lunch. The bagpiper felt bad for being late, and apologized to the men. He then went to the side of the grave and looked down and saw that the vault lid was already in place. He didn't know what else to do, so he started to play. The workers put down their lunches and began to gather around. The bagpiper played his heart and soul out for this man with no family or friends. He played like he'd never played before for this homeless man. As he played 'Amazing Grace' the workers began to cry. They wept, and he wept. They all wept together. When he finished, he packed his bagpipes and started walking to his car. Though his head was hung low, his heart was full. As he opened the door to his car he heard one of the workers say, 'I never seen anything like that before, and I've been putting in septic tanks for twenty years.'"

All four were laughing so hard that the coffee sloshed out of the carafe sitting on the table. After a couple of minutes laughing, and with tears rolling down his cheeks Bert said, "That makes two of your best we've heard this afternoon, Fred. I think Kyle and I will get back over to the Sheriff's Department. Thanks for the uplift."

Kyle echoed Bert's remarks, and the two said bye's to Raymond and departed.

Fred then said, "Raymond, I appreciate so much your updating us on the big trip. It sounds like everything is coming together real good. I hope you will continue to keep us posted as you learn anything new about the trip."

"Sure will, Fred," Raymond replied. "Talking about it helps me to prepare mentally for it. I appreciate you all listening to me."

Raymond and Fred shook hands, and Raymond left for his church.

Chapter 9

Harlan County, Kentucky

Fatso was sitting in his usual spot, at the checkout counter at Maggard's grocery. He was engrossed reading a novel and didn't notice the car pull into the parking lot in front of the store. He heard the door open and looked up and saw Pretty Boy Maggard walk in. Fatso's eyes got very large. He stood and said, "As I live and breathe . . . is it a ghost, or is it really Pretty Boy Maggard?"

"It is I," said Pretty Boy. "Good to see you Fatso. You haven't changed a bit in thirteen years. I had a little business in Knoxville and just thought I'd drive up to pay you and Trigger a visit."

Fatso replied, "You still living in Columbia.....way down there in South America?"

"Still there," replied Pretty Boy. "I don't really have much choice. The law wouldn't think kindly of me being here in the states, if you know what I mean."

"Yeah, I know," Fatso said. Fatso noticed that Pretty Boy apparently still had the bad habit of chewing tobacco. Tobacco stained streaks were still obvious from each side of his mouth extending down to his chin.

"Is ole Trigger in," asked Pretty Boy.

"He sure is, and I know he'll be surprised and glad to see you," Fatso replied. "Say, Pretty Boy, you know what they call elephants that ride on trains?"

Pretty Boy said, "Press the button, Fatso"

"They call them passengers!" Fatso replied, and pressed the button to open the back door into Trigger's office.

Trigger was sitting at his desk getting ready to use the phone when the door opened and in walked Pretty Boy. Normally he would have seen him in the parking lot or in the grocery store by viewing the monitors in his office that were hooked up to remote cameras, but he had just gone to the bathroom and returned to his desk.

"Office looks about like I left it thirteen years ago," said Pretty Boy as he stuck out his hand to Trigger.

Trigger shook his hand and said, "What a surprise. I didn't know if I would ever see you again Pretty Boy. Did the governor issue you a pardon or something?"

"You know better than that," Pretty Boy replied. "As I just told Fatso, I had a little business in Knoxville and just decided to drive up to Harlan to see you two.....just for ole times sake."

"Well have a seat, and let's talk," Trigger replied.

Pretty Boy pulled up a chair in front of Trigger's desk and said, "You got a cup or something I can spit in?"

Trigger pulled out a couple of Kleenex and stuffed them into a Styrofoam cup and handed it to Pretty Boy. "Still chewing, I see."

Pretty Boy spit a long streak of tobacco juice into the cup and said, "Yeah, nasty habit, but one of my few pleasures these days." A few drops started their journey from each edge of his mouth toward his chin.

Trigger said, "So what kind of business you got going in Knoxville these days, if it's any of my business?"

"Hey Trigger, we're ole buddies," Pretty Boy said. "I don't mind telling you. Course you know I'm in business in Columbia with our old army buddies Sam and Jose. We're doing great in the drug trade. But Columbia has another crop that's worth a lot of money, and that's coffee. Columbia and the U.S. tax the hell out of it when exported and imported, but we've found a way around that, and we're establishing a distribution system in the U.S. with wholesale coffee suppliers. Once it's set up we'll be able to ship hundreds of tons of coffee beans to them and bypass all the taxes. It should be a very profitable business."

"Never thought of you being in the coffee business, Pretty Boy," Trigger replied.

"Well, it's something new. Me, Sam, and Jose have high hopes for it. I'll keep you posted on how it goes," said Pretty Boy. "Is there anything I can do for you?"

Trigger thought for a moment, and then said, "As a matter of fact, I'm having a problem in supplying customers with guns. You got any of those for sale?"

"That's one of our specialties, Trigger, as I'm sure you recall from your six months with us. I could ship you a box of 100 pistols. It'd cost you $100 per gun, or $10,000. For that price the guns would still have their serial numbers on them. If you want them without serial numbers it will cost twice as much."

"I'll take one hundred with serial numbers," Trigger

replied. "I can take care of the serial numbers. I got a good supply of sulfuric acid, and Fatso knows how to use it to burn the numbers off. I suppose you want cash."

"Your memory is good. We still do only a cash-up-front business. It avoids a lot of problems," said Pretty Boy.

"How you going to make delivery?" asked Trigger.

"We have arrangements set up to get anything into Knoxville. I'll have a special courier drive them to you from there. You should have them in less than a month," Pretty Boy replied.

Trigger stood from behind his desk and turned to the picture on the wall behind him. He swung the picture on its hinges to reveal a wall safe behind it. He entered the combination, and then opened the safe. He then pulled out a large stack of $100 bills and started counting. When he reached $10,000 he placed the stack in a box and then handed it to Pretty Boy. "Feel free to count it," he said.

"I just did," said Pretty Boy as he took the box and placed it beside his chair. "Good to do business with you. You'll have your guns in short order." Pretty boy then spit another big streak of tobacco juice into the cup.

Trigger and Pretty Boy talked for another hour, getting caught up on everything.

Pretty Boy then stood up, stretched, and asked to use the bathroom. Afterwards, he shook hands with Trigger, grabbed his box of money, and said, "Been real good seeing you again my friend, and even good to see ole Fatso. Even though he's still at those corny elephant jokes!"

"Well, you can't teach an old dog new tricks, Pretty Boy," replied Trigger.

Pretty Boy said, "We'll keep in touch." And he turned and walked out the door into the grocery store.

On his way to the front door Pretty Boy shouted over at Fatso, "Good to see you again, Fatso. You take care."

Fatso replied, "Good to see you Pretty Boy. You know where baby elephants come from?"

No reply

"Baby elephants come from big storks," Fatso pronounced.

The door slammed.

Both Fatso and Trigger were watching on the monitors as Pretty Boy got in his car. They both thought it a bit strange that he turned the car right, toward Harlan, rather than left, toward Knoxville, when he pulled out of the parking lot.

Chapter 10

Victoria, Seychelles

The office was full. Bishop David Morgan was meeting with the six coordinators for the upcoming mission trip sponsored by the Catholic Church. The office was that of the Bishop, in the Cathedral of Immaculate Conception in Victoria. The Roman Catholic Diocese of Port Victoria was established on July 14, 1892.

Bishop Morgan had described the upcoming schedule. He had distributed paperwork that had the names of all the priests and pastors that would be participating, the pairings of one priest and one pastor, and the schedule of where each pair would be going, along with maps. Each coordinator knew the pair they were assigned to, and would now be working to complete the detailed schedule of whom they would meet, when, and how much time they would have at each stop. In addition, they would have to arrange sleeping accommodations and meals. Also, they would coordinate with each church or chapel at the five different locations to make sure each had scheduled for a two-hour service each evening. Lastly, they would provide all transportation for their team of ministers. It would certainly be a busy two weeks.

The coordinators were all Catholic priests from churches in or around Victoria, and were very familiar with the Seychelles. The population of greater Victoria is about twenty-five thousand, and the total population of the Seychelles around ninety thousand.

Each coordinator was told the anticipated arrival time of their ministers at the Victoria airport, and they were expected to meet those flights and take them to the hotel in Victoria that would be their residence for the two nights prior to their starting their scheduled visits. After the ministers got a good night's rest, the coordinator would spend the first day going over the two week agenda with them, taking them on a sightseeing trip of Victoria, providing them three good meals, and answering any questions they might have. Then the following morning they would be off to the first of five two-day visits.

Peter Alexander noticed that he had been assigned as coordinator to a Catholic priest from Chicago, whose name was Father Elmer Schmidt, and to a Baptist minister from Harlan, Kentucky, whose name was Pastor Raymond Bell. Peter's first thoughts were that he was indeed familiar with Chicago, having attended a conference there recently. He was not familiar with Harlan, although he did know that the University of Kentucky usually had a good basketball team. He looked forward to meeting and spending the two weeks with Father Schmidt and Pastor Bell.

Peter then heard the Bishop ask if any of the coordinators had questions. All did, and the meeting lasted about another hour. The meeting then concluded, and each coordinator began the task of filling in all the details for the two week mission trip that was just about one month off.

Chapter 11

Harlan, Kentucky

"Bert and Kyle, Bert and Kyle," Polly squawked as the sheriff and his deputy entered Creech Cafe and headed for a table toward the back. Fred was pouring coffee for customers at the counter, and when finished walked over, filled cups for Bert and Kyle, and sat down to join them. "Good to see the law once again patrolling in my humble establishment," he said.

"Morning Fred," responded both Bert and Kyle.

"Anything new in our fair city that we should know about?" asked Bert.

Fred replied, "Not much. I had a meeting last night with the city council. The subject of tourism came up again ... that's a popular topic these days, since tourists in our town bring in bucks. The thing that was on their collective minds last night was the small number of people visiting the Seibert Anchor Cross memorial."

Fred was referring to the one million dollar memorial that was built on the court house grounds from a portion of the funds recovered in the attempted bank robbery of thirteen years ago. The memorial was a small building constructed on the Northwest corner of the court house property. It was built to allow visitors to come into the structure and see photographs and read articles about all the events that occurred, and read about the history of the Seibert Anchor Cross, largely as established through the research of Dr. Randy Peters, Director of the University of Kentucky's Center for Appalachian Research.

Fred continued, "The thing is, only tourists would have an interest in visiting the memorial. All the home town people have already seen it, and it's pretty much a one-time thing, unless relatives come to visit and they want to take them to see it. Otherwise, tourists are its only visitors, and we just don't have a lot of them. So the council members wanted to do something to stir up interest with the memorial to bring in a fresh flood of tourists."

"So did you think of any way to do that?" asked Kyle.

Fred said, "I think the consensus was that without actually having the Seibert Anchor Cross there to see it would be difficult to lure tourists."

"Well, one big problem with that is the value of the artifact. It would be almost impossible to have enough security to assure its safety. The thing is truly priceless. Even just melting it down and selling it for the value of the gold would bring over a million dollars," Bert commented. "That's too much temptation for crooks to resist."

"Yeah, even the council realized that," Fred responded. "So the only thing any of us could come up with was to see if Dr. Peters might agree to bring it back to Harlan and display it in the memorial maybe for a weekend. It could be in observance of an anniversary date, or something like that. If we could get the media to cover it big time we might well attract a lot of attention and tourists. And we could manage big time security for a couple of days"

"So what did you decide to do?" Kyle asked.

Fred said, "They directed me to contact Randy to explore if that might be a possibility. So I plan to give him a call to discuss it."

"Good, keep us posted," Bert replied.

"We need some cheer this morning, Fred, you got any new wall postings you would share with us?" asked Kyle.

Fred rubbed his chin for a moment, and then pointed to a newspaper article on the wall not far from their table and said, "You see that one over there? The one with the picture of the big Labrador retriever."

Bert and Kyle nodded in agreement.

Fred continued, "Well, I put that one up about a week ago. Course, it was an article in the Harlan **Enterprise**, which you fellows seldom find time to read. The headline with the picture of the dog read 'Talking Dog'. Turns out this old mountaineer about 10 miles north of Evarts owned the dog. A salesman was driving by and saw a hand lettered sign in the yard 'Talking Dog for Sale' and he just had to stop and inquire. He knocked on the door and the mountaineer told him the dog was in the back yard. The salesman walks around to the back of the house and sees the dog sitting there. 'You talk,' he asks. 'Yep,' the dog replies. After the salesman recovers from the shock of hearing the dog talk he says, 'So, what's your story?' The dog looks up and says, 'Well, I discovered that I could talk when I was pretty young. I wanted to help the government, so I told the CIA. In no time they had me jetting from country to country, sitting in rooms with spies and world leaders, because no one figured a dog would be eavesdropping. I was one of their most valuable spies for eight years. But the jetting around really tired me out, and I knew I wasn't getting any younger so I decided to settle down. I signed up for a job at the airport to do some undercover security, wandering near suspicious characters and listening in. I uncovered some incredible dealings and was awarded a bunch of medals. I got married, had a lot of puppies, and now I'm just retired.' The salesman is amazed. He walks back to the front of the house and sees the mountaineer in a rocking chair on the front porch smoking a pipe. The salesman asks the mountaineer, 'How much you want for that dog?' 'Ten dollars,' the mountaineer replies. 'Ten dollars? That dog is incredible. Why on earth are you selling him so cheap?' asks the salesman. The mountaineer replies, 'Because he's a bullshitter. He's never been out of the back yard.'"

Bert and Kyle both burst out laughing, and continued for a good while. Finally Bert said, "Fred, you sure can tell a story. I think that one will carry me through the rest of the day."

"I'm sure it will for me too. That was a good one," added Kyle.

Just as Bert and Kyle were standing to leave, Pastor Bell entered and rushed over to their table. "I caught the three of you. Just who I wanted to talk to. You got one more minute?" asked Raymond.

"Sure," the three said in unison, and all sat back down.

Raymond continued, "I stopped by the Sheriff's Department, but Rosie said you two were getting a cup of coffee over here, and I wanted to talk with Fred too, so this works out perfectly. Betty and I would like to invite you three to dinner at our house this Friday evening. It's sort of a farewell party, since she will be leaving on Monday for Florida for a couple of weeks with relatives, and I'll be leaving Saturday for the Seychelles on my two week mission trip. I sure hope you can all make it."

All three nodded in agreement. Fred said, "Wouldn't miss it for the world."

Raymond added, "Oh, and Bert, please ask Carolyn if she can make it also, and we've already invited Randy Peters. He said he would be there, and agreed to spend Friday evening with us before returning to Lexington on Saturday. Betty will have a good meal for us, and it should be a lot of fun."

Fred said, "Betty's meals are always special, and to get

together with all our friends is always a treat as well. Thanks so much for the invitation, Raymond."

Raymond said, "Good, then I hope to see you all Friday around seven."

Fred added, "Raymond, one more thing before you leave. I just remembered that new picture you see there behind you on the wall . . . the one that looks like it was taken at a cemetery. I just put it up there a couple of days ago. Would you allow me to tell you the story behind it?"

Bert, Kyle, and Raymond grinned and got comfortable in their chairs.

Fred began, "The picture was taken at an old family cemetery about half way between here and Cumberland. The story goes that there was a big, old walnut tree just inside the cemetery fence. One day two boys filled up a bucketful of walnuts and sat down beside the tree, out of sight, and began dividing up the nuts. 'One for you, one for me, one for you, one for me', said one boy. Several of the nuts dropped and rolled down toward the fence. Another boy came along riding his bike along the road beside the cemetery. As he passed he thought he heard voices from inside the cemetery. He stopped to investigate. Sure enough, he heard, 'One for you, one for me, one for you, one for me . . . ' He just knew what it was. He jumped back on his bike and rode off. Just around the bend he met an old man with a cane hobbling along. 'Come here quick,' said the boy, 'You won't believe what I just heard! The Lord and Satan are down at the cemetery dividing up the souls!' The man said, 'Beat it kid, can't you see it's hard for me to walk.' When the boy insisted, the man hobbled slowly to the cemetery. Standing by the fence they heard, 'One for you, one for me, one for you, one for me . . . ' The old man whispered, 'Boy, you've been telling me the truth. Let's see if we can see the Lord . . . ' Shaking with fear, they peered through the fence, yet were still unable to see anything. The old man and the boy gripped the wrought iron bars of the fence tighter and tighter as they tried to get a glimpse of the Lord. At last they heard, 'One for you, and one for me, That's all. Now let's go get those nuts by the fence and we'll be done'. They say the old man had the lead for a good half-mile before the kid on the bike passed him!"

Roars of laughter emanated from the table.

Bert then said, "I feel good enough now to maybe work about halfway through the second shift! Thanks, Fred."

Kyle replied, "Yeah, that was a real lift. But I think I'll quit after the first shift!"

Raymond said, "I'll try and remember that one to tell some of the folks on my trip. Thanks Fred, see you all Friday at seven."

Chapter 12

Harlan County, Kentucky

Eagle Eye Looney lived in a house on a small family farm not far from the community of Cawood, Kentucky. Cawood is about ten miles south of the town of Harlan on Highway 421. The Looneys had farmed the land there for several generations. Eagle Eye was one of four brothers. The other three were reasonably diligent and hard working. Eagle Eye was not. He had attracted trouble all his life. He had gotten his nickname Eagle Eye because of his ability to shoot a gun very accurately. He had served in the army, and had wound up as a sniper. He was an expert marksman. He was always looking for a quick buck, and it mattered little if getting it involved something illegal. He had served several jail sentences, but presently was out and just laying around the house watching television, trying to think of yet another way to turn a quick buck. His parents were deceased, and his three brothers were all working. He thought he heard a car drive up to the house.

"Anybody home?" shouted Pretty Boy Maggard.

Eagle Eye got up off the couch and walked to the screened door. He looked out and saw a stranger standing beside his car. The man looked very well dressed, and well groomed. What looked out of place was the tobacco juice stains flowing down from each side of his mouth toward his chin. The man then spit a large streak of tobacco juice and repeated, "Anybody home I say?"

"Who wants to know," Eagle Eye replied, and opened the screen door and walked slowly onto the front porch.

Pretty Boy walked onto the porch and stuck out his hand, "You might not remember me Eagle Eye. My name is Pretty Boy Maggard. Several years back I operated Maggard's Grocery down around Wallins. I remember when you got in a bit of trouble after buying a gun from me and getting caught trying to hold-up a store in the mall."

"You got a pretty good memory," Eagle Eye said. "Yeah,

now that I think about it, I do remember buying that gun from you, although I think it was Fatso Chapel that actually sold it to me. I thought you got in a bunch of trouble when they found several million dollars of drug money in your lock boxes and you left the country. Are you back?"

"Just on a business trip, Eagle Eye," replied Pretty Boy. "And part of that business involves you, if you're interested in earning $10,000."

Eagle Eye's eyes got big as saucers, and his mouth dropped open. "Yes sir, indeed I am interested in earning ten big ones. Come over here and have a seat and tell me all about what you've got in mind." Eagle Eye had a seat in the swing and pointed to a chair for Pretty Boy.

Pretty Boy slowly tested the chair before putting his full weight into it, and then said, "Well, it goes something like this. About thirteen years ago Sheriff J. Bert Sterling caused me a lot of trouble. I'm interested in getting a little revenge."

"How you think you gonna do that?" asked Eagle Eye.

"Reports I get say you know how to handle a gun," said Pretty Boy. "So I just thought you might be interested in giving our ole Harlan County Sheriff a little lead poisoning."

"Possibly, possibly," Eagle Eye said slowly. "I think if I had

$10,000 in cash I could think real strong on how I might be able to bring that about."

"I sort of thought you might see it that way," said Pretty Boy. "You could do it any way you wanted, and I'm not in any big hurry. You could take your time and figure out how to do it such that you were in the clear. I'm sure you're not wanting to spend any more time in the big house."

"You got that right," Eagle Eye replied. "I've had enough of that. Man can do a whole lot of plotting about something with $10,000."

Pretty Boy slowly got up out of his chair and walked off the porch to his car. He opened the door and reached inside and brought out a box. He carried the box back on the porch and again took a seat. He then slowly took the top off the box and held it so that Eagle Eye could see inside it. "There's $10,000 there Eagle Eye," Pretty Boy said with a sly smile on his face.

"Looks about right," Eagle Eye replied.

"So let me just make sure we have a real clear understanding," Pretty Boy said. "You accept this money I'm expecting to read Sheriff J. Bert Sterling's obit in the Harlan **Enterprise.** I'll give you a month to make that happen. If it doesn't happen I'll send out a guy that will make absolutely certain your obit will make the paper. Are we clear?"

Eagle Eye replied, "Crystal clear. You can count on me."

Pretty Boy then said, "Deal" And handed Eagle Eye the box.

Eagle Eye took the box, flipped through the cash, then stuck out a hand to Pretty Boy. The two shook hands slowly, with their eyes glowing at each other.

Pretty Boy turned and walked to his car, got in and drove off. As he was driving back to Knoxville he thought all had turned out exactly as he had hoped . . . actually even better. He had not planned on getting the $10,000 dollars from Trigger Green for the guns. When he did he immediately decided that it would be what he would offer Eagle Eye Looney to take care of Sheriff Sterling. Otherwise, he would have been required to have a courier deliver the cash back to Eagle Eye from Knoxville. But this was much better, since getting that much cash back through security at the airport could also have been a problem. Sometimes you get lucky, he thought. Ole sheriff J. Bert Sterling is good as dead.

Chapter 13

Victoria, Mahe Island, Seychelles

Father Peter Alexander was in his study at the Cathedral of Immaculate Conception in Victoria. He was preparing to leave to visit the last of the five sites that his pair of ministers would visit, starting next Tuesday. He had visited the sites in reverse order. He started on North Island, then went to Silhouette Island, then to Beau Villon and Anse Boileau, both on Mahe. The last stop would be a visit to the Faure Plantation, located on the Northeast coast of Mahe. He would drive north on the North Coast road for a distance of only about five miles from Victoria. The Faure Plantation was close to the Maidive Village. Because the Faure Plantation was quite extensive, and employed hundreds of workers, there was a chapel located there for the worship convenience of the workers. Father Alexander planned to make arrangements at several establishments in Maidive Village for his two ministers to visit, and then he would drive to the plantation and meet with the priest there to work out the details for the two evening services the visiting ministers would conduct. The plantation owner, Felix Faure, also planned to meet with them at the chapel.

Felix Faure was a sixth generation Faure owner of the plantation. His great, great, great, great grandfather, Jean-Paul Faure had begun the plantation operation in 1820. Felix was now sixty-five years old, and had two sons and two daughters. All of his children were very interested and active in the operation of the plantation, so it looked as though the Faure ownership would likely continue. Felix, like his father, grandfather, and other ancestors was a very good and fair owner. His workers liked him very much, and worked hard to please him. Also like his ancestors, he was a highly religious person. He was a devout Christian, and had tried to lead many of his workers to Christ. He maintained a chapel on the plantation property that had first been established by the founder, Jean-Paul Faure, in 1855. It was operated by the Catholic church, and a priest, Father Morgan, from nearby Maidive Village came to the chapel each Sunday to conduct services. The chapel was normally near capacity for these services. It held about one hundred persons.

Upon entering the vestibule of the chapel one first noticed a beautiful wooden anchor cross displayed in a large cabinet. The anchor cross itself was only about six-inches-high and about four-inches-across, and was displayed at a height of about five-feet in its cabinet. Only the wooden face of the anchor cross was visible through the thick glass in the top, front of the cabinet. It was placed in a cutout of marble stone that only allowed the wooden surface of the anchor cross to be seen. The piece of marble rested on a shelf in the cabinet, which extended to the floor. There was a plaque attached to the outside of the cabinet under the anchor cross that read:

This beautiful anchor cross was brought ashore on the Faure Plantation in 1860 by two sailors that had been adrift for 3 days in the Indian Ocean after their ship, *The Aqaba Maiden*, had sunk after striking a coral reef in a storm. They were the only known survivors, and attributed being saved to the power of Christ as represented by this anchor cross. These two were called "Red" and "Bones". They worked

faithfully on the Faure Plantation until they went to be with their Lord. Following their passing, this chapel was dedicated as The Red Bones Chapel on October 9, 1925.

Known only to Felix Faure, Father Morgan, and select of the Faure family, there was a sliding panel on the back side of the cabinet that could only be opened by pressing a button on the top right side of the cabinet. The button was under a small piece of the cabinet wood that could slide upward to reveal the button. By pressing the button and simultaneously sliding the panel the back side of the anchor cross could be accessed, and pulled free from its marble enclosure. This arrangement of the anchor cross in the cabinet was to assure that anyone viewing the anchor cross did not see its golden back side. The Faures were afraid that someone might attempt to steal the anchor cross if they were aware that it contained so much pure gold. The cabinet was thus designed to conceal the gold, to show only the wooden side.

Father Alexander arrived at the Red Bones Chapel at precisely the scheduled appointment time of 3 pm. He had just come from several establishments in Maidive Village where he arranged for his two ministers to visit next Wednesday and Thursday. Now he was to meet with Father Morgan and Felix

Faure here at the chapel to assure everything was all set for the evening services.

The door to the chapel was standing open, and as Father Alexander started up the stairs two gentlemen walked out the door to greet him.

"Father Alexander, I presume. I'm Father Morgan and this is Felix Faure, owner of the plantation," Father Morgan pronounced as everyone shook hands.

"Please, please, do come on in, and welcome to the Red Bones Chapel," said Felix Faure.

"It is most impressive," said Father Alexander as the three of them entered the vestibule. Father Alexander immediately focused on the very beautiful wooden anchor cross in its elaborate cabinet just in front of them, and said, "Oh my, what a wonderful and beautiful wooden anchor cross. I have never seen one like it," and he read the inscription on the attached plaque. "And such a history," he said after reading it. "I was never aware of it, and I live in Victoria, only a few miles from here."

"It is very impressive and historical," said Felix Faure. "Most of those that see it are workers here on the plantation, so it's fame has not spread widely," he said with a grin.

"Shall we take a look at the chapel?" offered Father Morgan

"By all means," said Father Alexander.

The three spent the next hour going over the plans for the two services to be held in the chapel at 7 pm on Wednesday and Thursday nights of next week. Father Morgan and Felix Faure assured Father Alexander that they would announce next week's services during the regular Sunday services and would also post announcements around the plantation. When all the questions were answered, good-byes were said and Father Alexander departed to return to Victoria. As he drove back he thought about his visit to the Red Bones Chapel. That wooden anchor cross was truly beautiful, and what a great history it had ..... going all the way back to 1860 when two sailors brought it ashore from a shipwreck! And the chapel there was very lovely. He was looking forward greatly to the services there next week.

Chapter 14

Harlan County, Kentucky

Eagle Eye Looney had not slept well last night. And that was very unusual. Normally he was either too drunk to remember when he went to bed, or he just dozed off watching television and when he woke up it was morning and the television was still blasting. His brothers tried to just ignore him . . . they had given up on being able to make him change his ways. Last night was different. After the visit from Pretty Boy Maggard he stashed the box of cash in his locker that was in his bedroom, and then went out to do a little celebrating. But even after having several drinks, when he came home around two in the morning he still couldn't sleep. He knew Pretty Boy meant what he said. If he didn't eliminate the sheriff he could expect a visit from a very serious hit man. He lay awake until morning thinking of how he could best take care of the sheriff. After considering several different methods, he finally decided on using a pistol at close range. Although he was an accomplished sniper, it was just too difficult to get a good shot using a rifle from a distance, and to even try that meant he would need to know exactly where the sheriff would be at a certain time and he would need to position himself in a hidden location, and that was always a problem. If he used a pistol at short range he was sure to take ole Bert out. That's what he'd do. Only problem was he didn't have a pistol. Since they caught him in that attempted robbery the law confiscated all his weapons, pistols and rifles. He didn't even have a shotgun for hunting. But he knew where he could get a pistol.

●●●

Fatso Chapel looked up from watching the small television on the checkout counter when he heard the doorbell cling.

"My, my, my. If it isn't ole Eagle Eye," Fatso said. "And I'm a poet and don't know it!

Eagle Eye responded, "Hey Fatso? Long time, no see."

"Yeah, I guess the last time I saw you was when you came in here several years back to buy that pistol that you got caught with when you tried to stick-up the store up at the mall, if my memory serves me correctly," Fatso replied.

"Yeah, that's right," Eagle Eye said. "You got a repeat customer . . . guess that means I approve of your business."

"You telling me you want another piece," Fatso said.

Eagle Eye replied, "That's exactly what I'm telling you, Fatso."

"You going to try another robbery? I'd think you would have learned your lesson from the last time," said Fatso.

"No, I've got other fish to fry this time. No robbery. You got a gun for me or not?" asked Eagle Eye.

"Well, we can possibly do some business, Eagle Eye, but we're running real low on pistols right now. We got another order coming in before long, but if you have to have one right now the price is going to be a little stiff. Supply and demand, you know," said Fatso.

"How much?" asked Eagle Eye.

"500 smacks," said Fatso. "Cash on the barrel head, so to speak."

"That's about twice the going rate, but I need it. So, okay, let's do it," Eagle Eye replied.

"Hold on a minute, I've got to get Trigger's okay. You just have a seat over there and I'll go back and see if the man approves the sale," Fatso said. "By the way, do you know what the banana said to the elephant, Eagle Eye?"

"No, and I really don't care. Would you please just run the deal by Trigger," said Eagle Eye.

"Don't be so pushy," Fatso said. "The banana didn't say anything to the elephant....banana's can't talk." Fatso said with a giggle as he pressed the button under his counter to open the door to Trigger's office. He then walked back and went in.

"What's up Fatso, I thought I saw you talking to Eagle Eye Looney out there," Trigger said.

"Yeah, and he wants to buy a pistol. I told him it'd be $500 cash, and he agreed. Okay with you?" asked Fatso.

"Well, we're down to five pistols, but $500 is a good price, and we should have that shipment from Pretty Boy in a few weeks, so yeah, go ahead and let him have one. I'll get it for you." Trigger got up from his desk and walked to a cabinet, unlocked it, and removed a pistol. Fatso noticed the other four in there as well as several rifles.

"Old Eagle Eye is pretty loose with his tongue," Trigger said. "Try and find out why he wants the pistol . . . I'd like to know what he's up to."

"I'll do it," said Fatso. "I asked him if he was going to try and stick-up another store, and he said no, he had other fish to fry. I'll try and see if I can get it out of him."

Fatso took the pistol, put it in his pocket, and walked back into the grocery store to the check-out counter. Eagle Eye stood up and walked over to the counter.

"Well?" asked Eagle Eye.

"The man said it would be okay, but he was glad to hear you weren't going to try another stick-em up," Fatso replied.

"Well, I told you I wouldn't be doing that. This time I got me a real profitable little job just to do some lead poisoning, if you know what I mean," Eagle Eye said with lifted eyebrows.

"Who's going to have the pleasure of getting the lead poisoning, Eagle Eye?" Fatso asked.

"Well, I don't want to brag, but I know you and Trigger will keep a lid on this. I'm going to get a little revenge for a feller against our fair sheriff," Eagle Eye replied.

"Sounds serious, Eagle Eye," Fatso replied. "You better watch your step, Bert's not an easy target."

"We'll see about that," said Eagle Eye. "Just give me the gun."

"Not so fast. Let's see the $500 first," said Fatso.

Eagle Eye reached into his pocket and pulled out a roll of one hundred-dollar bills, and peeled off five of them, and laid them on the counter.

Fatso reached into his pocket and removed the pistol and placed it in a grocery bag.

Fatso picked up the money and said, "Good to do business with you Eagle Eye. You better be real careful."

Eagle Eye took the grocery bag with the pistol in it and turned to leave.

"You know where you find elephants, Eagle Eye?" asked Fatso.

Eagle Eye continued to walk to the front door.

"It depends on where you lost them," replied Fatso with a grin and a chuckle.

The front door slammed.

Fatso then walked back into Trigger's office.

"So, did you find out what he's up to?" asked Trigger.

"Yeah, and you're not going to like it," responded Fatso. "He told me he plans to take out the sheriff."

"That guy's a real nut," replied Trigger. "He can handle a gun, but he can't handle his mouth or his brain . . . if he has one. This does present a problem for us. We're always on the other side of the law, but Sheriff Sterling is a straight shooter and I have a lot of respect for him. Any other sheriff might be a lot more of a problem for us than Bert. But I can't just go to him and say that there's a contract out for him and Eagle Eye is the hit man. That would ruin our reputation, and be bad for business."

Fatso responded, "I hear you. I like Bert too. So what're you going to do?"

"I got to think a bit about it, but I'm inclined to give the sheriff a bit of a warning without revealing Eagle Eye. Bert's pretty good at taking care of himself," Trigger said.

"Wonder who hired Eagle Eye?" asked Fatso

"My guess would be Pretty Boy. I wondered why after he finished visiting with us he turned his car toward Harlan rather than back toward Knoxville. I'd be willing to bet he headed straight for Cawood to proposition Eagle Eye," Trigger said.

"You're probably right. What do you do when an elephant sneezes?" asked Fatso.

"Get back to work Fatso," replied Trigger.

"You get out of the way," Fatso said with a giggle as he turned and went back into the grocery store.

Chapter 15

Harlan, Kentucky

It was getting late on Thursday afternoon. The day had been pretty routine for Sheriff J. Bert Sterling. He was at his desk doing some paperwork when Rosie called him on the intercom.

"Yes Rosie," Bert said.

"Mr. Trigger Green is here to see you Sheriff," Rosie replied.

Bert dropped the pen he was writing with, and wondered what the occasion might be that would bring Trigger to his office. It was rare indeed when a known crook voluntarily visited the law.

"Please send him in, Rosie," replied the sheriff.

The door to the sheriff's office opened and Trigger Green walked in.

"Mr. Green, please do come in and have a seat. Can I get you something to drink . . . non-alcoholic of course," Bert greeted.

"Afternoon Bert, no thanks, I'm good. I just wanted to chat with you for a moment if you're not too tied up," Trigger replied.

"Absolutely, and what are we talking about?" Bert asked.

Trigger replied, "Well, this is a bit tricky. Let me start by saying that I've got the utmost respect for you. I know we play on different sides of the court, so to speak, but you've always been upfront and fair with me. I don't have any desire to see you get hurt."

Bert said, "Is there something I don't know about?"

"My guess would be that there is," Trigger replied. "I'm not at liberty to discuss any names, but I have good reason to believe that there is a contract out on you."

Bert then said, "Oh boy, that's not good news. Can you tell me anything more about this contract?"

"Like I said, I've got to be careful," Trigger replied. "I can tell you that a certain Harlan County low-life has apparently been given a bunch of money and he's running around saying that he's been hired to take care of Sheriff J. Bert Sterling. He's certainly not the smartest person in the county, but he does know how to handle a gun. I just wanted to give you a heads-up so you can be a little extra cautious. Like I said, I really don't want to see you get hurt."

"I appreciate that Trigger. And I agree with you, I really don't want to be hurt," Bert said with a grin. "I will try and be a little extra cautious. Do you have any idea when this should come down?"

"That I really don't know, but I suspect pretty soon," replied Trigger.

Trigger stood up and reached across the desk to shake Bert's hand and said, "Watch your back." He then turned to walk out of the office.

"Thanks again, Trigger, I really do appreciate your concern and the warning. I'll do my best to dodge the bullet." the sheriff said as Trigger left his office.

●●●

Kyle and Rosie had already left the office for the day, and Deputy Mousy Giles had arrived for the second shift about half an hour ago. Bert walked out of his office toward the front door. When he got to the door he reached up and gave Preacher Puss a nice pet, and the cat responded appreciatively with a big meow and swish of her tail.

"I'm going to call it a day, Mousy, I think I'll go across the street and get one last cup of coffee before I go home. Hold down the fort, and don't let the crooks take over," Bert said, and then headed for Creech Cafe.

"Here's the law, here's the law," Polly squawked as Bert walked in.

"At ease Polly," Bert replied and gave the bird a stroke before walking to the counter and sitting on a stool.

Fred appeared as if by magic and said, "About time for you to head home for the day isn't it sheriff?"

"After I drink one last cup of coffee that's exactly what I plan to do Fred," Bert replied. "But I did want to run something by you to get your take on it.....is your clock running?"

"I'm all ears," Fred said as he poured Bert a steaming cup of coffee.

Bert started, "I had a visit this afternoon from Trigger

Green. That alone is very, very unusual. But the purpose of Trigger's visit was to give me a tip that someone had placed a contract on me. Course he wouldn't tell me who it was, or who the hit man was, but he seemed genuinely concerned, and just said he wanted to give me a heads-up to watch my back."

Fred answered, "That really sounds heavy. Maybe you need to have Kyle stick real close to you. Four eyes are better than two."

"Yeah, I had thought of that, and I'm going to talk tomorrow with Kyle about it. I really don't know anything to do other than to try and be a little more cautious. Being the mayor of our fair city, I just wanted to tell you about it. I think it best that the word not spread, but I know there are lots of locals that come in here to talk and you might hear something that could be useful. So I'm just asking if you'd mind keeping your ears open, and let me know if you hear anything that sounds suspicious," Bert said.

Fred then said, "My good friend, you know I'll do anything at all to help you. I consider you my very best friend. My ears will be wide open, and I'll let you know the minute I hear anything. You just be extra cautious, and you inform Kyle and make sure he sticks close to you."

"Thanks, Fred," Bert replied. "I knew I could count on you. And what you said about my being your best friend applies for me as well.....you're the best."

"Well, after all that sad news I think you need something to cheer you up on your way home," Fred said.

"I bet I'm getting ready to hear one," Bert replied with a big grin.

Fred began, "This one is a true story, and I found it in a 'Law and Order' magazine. It's posted on the wall over there behind that table. A husband went to the sheriff's office to report that his wife was missing. The conversation went something like this:

husband: My wife is missing, She went shopping yesterday and
      didn't come home.

deputy: What is her height?

husband: Gee, I'm not sure. A little-over five-feet I think

deputy: Weight?

husband: Don't know for sure. Not slim, but not fat.

deputy: Color of eyes?

husband: Never noticed.

deputy: Color of hair?

husband: Changes fairly frequently. Maybe brown right now.

deputy: What was she wearing?

husband: Could have been a skirt or pants. I'm not sure.

deputy: What kind of car was she driving?

husband: Didn't go in a car, she took my pick up truck.

deputy: What kind of a truck was it?

Husband: Brand new Ford F150 King Ranch 4X4 with eco-boost 5.0L V8 engine special ordered with manual transmission. It has a custom matching white cover for the bed. Custom leather seats and "Bubba" floor mats. Trailering package with gold hitch. DVD with navigation, twenty-one-channel CB radio, six cup holders, and four power outlets. Added special alloy wheels and off-road Michelins. Wife put a small scratch on the driver's door.

At this point the husband started choking up.

deputy: Don't worry buddy, we'll find your truck."

Bert and Fred both laughed a good while, and then Bert said, "Well, Fred, that one should keep me in a good mood for the rest of the day. Appreciate it."

Fred replied, "Laughter is good for the soul, my friend. Have a good evening, and I'll look forward to seeing you and the gang at the Bell's tomorrow evening for dinner."

"Yes indeed, it should be a great evening," replied Bert as he left for home.

Chapter 16

Harlan County, Kentucky

For the second night in a row, Eagle Eye had problems sleeping. He woke early on Friday morning. He had set his alarm clock for 5 am, but awoke before it went off. His brothers didn't normally get up until around 7 am, and he wanted to be gone before that. He had decided that the best way to take care of the sheriff would be to make the hit at his office. He knew that Bert normally arrived at his office early, usually around 7 am, and that Rosie and Kyle wouldn't arrive until shortly before 8 am. So his plan was simple. He would get to the Sheriff's Department at about 7:20 am, enter through the door that Bert always left unlocked after his arrival, and then walk through the reception area to Bert's office, open his door, and make the hit. He wasn't worried about anyone hearing the noise from the shot, since it would be inside the building. The plan sounded good to Eagle Eye. After his bathroom duties, he got dressed, got the gun out of his footlocker, and then went to the kitchen to get some breakfast. By 6:30 am he was on his way to Harlan.

Bert walked into his office just after 7 am. He had gotten a good night's rest, but had laid awake for a while thinking about Trigger's visit. He had decided to have a meeting first thing this morning with both Rosie and Kyle to inform them about the apparent contract that was out for him. And he knew that Kyle would insist on staying close with him to help watch for the hit man. Bert went to his coffee machine and got it going, and then sat at his desk and fired up his computer to see if he had any new email, and to check for any events that might have occurred overnight.

Eagle Eye arrived outside the Sheriff's Department on Central Street just in time to see the sheriff walking up to the front entrance and unlocking the door. Just as planned! He wanted to give him time to get settled in his office, so he parked and waited about twenty minutes. He checked his gun, made sure the safety was off, and went over the plan in his mind one last time. He looked all around before opening his car door to see if there was anyone in sight that might identify him. There was not. The time had arrived for him to earn his ten-grand. He opened the car door and started walking toward the Sheriff's Department.

He got to the entrance door and listened to see if he could detect any sound inside, in case the sheriff might be in the reception room. He heard nothing. He started turning the door knob, and then slowly started opening the door. As it opened he saw no one in the front office. He reached in his pocket and retrieved his pistol, and with it extended in front of him he started into the office. Big mistake! The next thing he was aware of was a loud scream, followed by something heavy landing atop his head. Long gray hair then flowed over his eyes, and the most excruciating pain he had ever felt came from around the top of his head. Blood poured down his face. He immediately dropped his gun and tried to reach up to knock off whatever was on his head, but just as he was swinging his hand up toward his head the weight was gone, and so was the hair covering his eyes. The blood, however, was still pouring down onto his face so he used his hand to wipe it from his eyes.

The door to the sheriff's office opened and Sheriff J. Bert Sterling was standing in the door with his pistol drawn and pointed directly at Eagle Eye.

"Don't even think about reaching down and getting that gun, Eagle Eye," Bert said.

The sheriff looked at the scene before him. Eagle Eye was standing there with blood streaked all over his face, and it was still dripping. His gun was lying on the floor at his feet. Preacher Puss was back on her shelf above the door, looking for all the world like she had just earned ten *Whisker Lickin* cat treats ..... swishing her tail and looking straight at Bert. Eagle Eye still did not know what had happened to him.

"Just stand real still, Eagle Eye, and put your hands behind your back. Don't twitch one muscle till I get these cuffs on you. One false move and I'll turn the monster back on you," Bert said as he retrieved his cuffs from his belt and placed them on Eagle Eye's wrists.

"Sheriff, I can't see," said Eagle Eye. "Got blood in both eyes . . . can you please wipe them for me."

With the handcuffs securely in place, Bert reached down and grabbed Eagle Eye's gun and stuck it under his belt and then said, "I'll take care of it. You sit there and I'll grab the first- aid kit."

Bert got the first-aid kit and applied bandages and cleaned Eagle Eye's face and eyes.

Bert then said, "A little bird told me there was a contract out for me, so now I guess I know who the hit man is. I suppose you wouldn't be interested in telling me who hired you?"

Eagle Eye responded, "Don't know what you're talking about Bert. I just came into town early this morning to get a head start doing some errands and I saw that pistol there in your belt just lying on the sidewalk outside Creech Cafe. As a law abiding citizen I felt it my duty to turn it in to you. Just after I opened the door and came in something attacked me. That's all I know."

"Surely you don't expect me to believe that story, Eagle Eye," Bert replied.

"Well, it's the gospel," replied Eagle Eye.

Bert then said, "We'll see what the judge has to say about that. And I happen to know that Judge Oakes is out of the office today and for the weekend. So you'll be our guest here in the slammer until Monday morning. It'll give you time to think about that story."

"I don't think it fair that I get put in jail for just trying to be a good citizen," said Eagle Eye. "What I'm going to be thinking about while I'm in there is suing the Sheriff's Department for all the pain and suffering I've endured due to whatever attacked me."

Bert said, "Good luck on that. I don't think even one of our low-life lawyers would take that case." He then took Eagle Eye to the holding cell.

A few minutes later Rosie arrived at the Sheriff's Department. Bert came out of his office and after greeting her, told her what had transpired earlier, and then told her as soon as Kyle got to the office for the two of them to please come into his office for a meeting.

Bert briefed Kyle and Rosie on both Trigger Green's visit and on Eagle Eye's attempted assassination this morning.

"Chalk up another win for Preacher Puss," Rosie exclaimed.

"Yeah, I'm beginning to wonder what that cat would look like wearing a deputy's uniform," Kyle added.

"She'd look real cute," Rosie said. "I think I might try and make her one."

Kyle said,"Seriously, Bert, this whole contracted hit thing

is something we've got to deal with. My guess is that Judge Oakes won't see enough evidence on Monday morning to hold Eagle Eye. And it is true he was attacked. I predict he'll be walking the streets fifteen minutes after his hearing."

Bert replied, "I agree one hundred percent. And the sad part is that whoever hired him will still be looking for him to complete the contract. I guess the only good news is that we now know Eagle Eye's the hit man. I really hate to tie you up with him Kyle, but I've been thinking that maybe you should tail him for a day or two after he gets out. What'd you think?"

Kyle said, "I agree. I think he's the only threat, so I wouldn't feel bad keeping an eye on him and not being with you. I'll be with him when he appears before the judge Monday morning, and I'll plan on trailing him when he leaves. I'll keep in touch, and you can let me know if anything new turns up."

Rosie then added, "Frankly, I'm concerned for both of you. Ole Eagle Eye's a real nut case, but he does know how to handle a gun. If he knew you were trailing him, Kyle, he'd likely try to do you in. And we know he's still going to be after Bert. How about asking one of our other deputies to work a little overtime for a few days till this whole thing blows over?"

"Not a bad idea, Rosie," the sheriff replied. "I'll ask Bill

Black if he'd consider working maybe 4 hours overtime each day for a while, starting on Monday. That way Bill could be available if needed and he could keep an eye on both Kyle and me."

"Good, that makes me feel better," Rosie replied.

All three then rose and walked back into the reception room. They all walked over beside the front door and looked up at Preacher Puss. The cat stared at the three of them, and then Rosie reached up with a handful of *Whisker Lickin* cat treats and laid them on the shelf. Bert then reached up and petted her while she ate her treats. She then laid down contentedly, closed her eyes, and began one of many morning cat naps.

•••

Eagle Eye's head was really hurting. He sat in his cell and tried to think about his situation. He figured Pretty Boy was not likely to hear about his botched hit this morning, but he knew he had to go to Plan B. He decided that the pistol thing wasn't such a good idea after all. And he was an expert sniper. He'd just have to get a good rifle and put together a plan to use it to take care of Bert.

Chapter 17

On Interstate 75 in Kentucky

Dr. Randy Peters was driving from Lexington to Harlan. He drove Interstate 75 from Lexington to Corbin, then exited onto Highway 25E to Pineville, then took Highway 119 to Harlan. It was about 150 miles, and usually took about three-hours. Randy always thought of the early pioneers as he made this journey. The route he followed was nearly the same as the one early settlers followed traveling through Cumberland Gap and then on into Kentucky. As he whizzed along at seventy miles per hour in his comfortable, air-conditioned car he thought of how much different the trip had been for the pioneers. Things had certainly changed.

Mayor Fred Knapp had called Randy a few days back and discussed with him the meeting that he had with the city council at which they requested the mayor to talk with Randy about the possibility of bringing the Seibert Anchor Cross to Harlan for a weekend's exhibit in the Seibert Anchor Cross memorial. After some discussion, Randy said he would be pleased to do so if Deputy Kyle Potter, who actually owned the artifact, was in agreement. Fred had then told Randy that perhaps they could talk about it with Kyle at the dinner tonight at the Bell's home. And so they would. Randy understood the council's desire to increase tourism in Harlan, but he still had strong memories from the ceremony last October 10th when he had the Pelle Anchor Cross there for display and the ceremony was disrupted by a large explosion. He certainly hoped if he brought the Seibert Anchor Cross for display things would go much smoother. But they could discuss that at dinner tonight. His thoughts then turned to Raymond and Betty Bell, and his friendship with them. He looked forward greatly to visiting them, and certainly to a fine meal. Betty was a superb cook!

● ● ●

Randy arrived in Harlan with about an hour to spare before the 7 pm dinner at the Bells. He figured that Fred Knapp would still be at Creech Cafe, and would likely go directly to dinner from there, so he thought he would stop by Creech's to visit a bit with Fred and then the two of them could go to the Bells together.

"Welcome, welcome, welcome," Polly greeted Randy as he entered Creech Cafe.

"Good to see you Polly," Randy said as he reached up and petted the bird.

"Well, well, well, I do believe it is the good Dr. Peters," Fred said from behind the counter. "Come in, come in, and have a seat over there. We'll have a cup of coffee together. We don't want to eat anything before that good meal we're going to have this evening."

Randy and Fred were seated at a table, and Fred poured them both a cup of coffee.

"I take it you just got into town a bit early and decided to stop by here to kill a little time," Fred said.

"Yeah, but I valued spending a bit of time with you Mr. Mayor," responded Randy. "Seems like we don't get to spend much time together these days, so I'm glad I arrived a bit early."

Randy and the mayor then spent the next forty-five minutes getting caught up. Randy then looked at his watch and said, "We've only about fifteen minutes to get to the Bells. You think we should be leaving?"

Fred responded, "Yeah, but it's only about ten minutes from here. Let me tell you my latest story . . . shouldn't take more than five minutes."

Randy grinned and said, "Fire away."

Fred responded, "Well, it's posted right there above your head on the wall. It was in yesterday's Harlan **Enterprise**. Headline read, 'Two men die in motorcycle crash'. These two guys were riding together on a motorcycle on 119 near the Harlan and Bell County line. One of the guys got cold, and they stopped and the cold one put on his jacket backwards so it would quit ballooning the air. They rode for another couple of miles and lost control and hit a tree. When the coroner arrived, he asked the rookie deputy if both men were dead when he arrived on the scene. He said one was, and by the time he got the head of the other one straightened out he was dead too."

After a period of laughter, Randy said, "I can't believe that actually happened."

"You're right," Fred said. "It was listed in the paper under 'funny stories.'"

"We've got just about ten minutes to make it to the Bell house," Fred said. "Let's head out."

•••

As they approached the Bell home they could smell the wonderful food being prepared for dinner. Fred and Randy stepped on the porch and rang the doorbell.

Betty Bell appeared at the door and said, "Welcome my friends, please do come in."

"Hi Betty, so good of you to invite us," Fred said.

Randy hugged Betty and said, "Always an honor to be in your home. Really appreciate you and Raymond."

Betty replied, "I think you're the last two to arrive, and I think you know everyone. Please be seated and I'll go back to the kitchen. Carolyn and I are putting on the finishing touches. We'll serve dinner in about a half hour."

"Smelling all those wonderful aromas will have my stomach more than ready in a half hour," replied Fred as he and Randy shook hands with Raymond, Kyle and Bert, and they all took a seat.

Fred thought he would take the opportunity to ask Kyle if he would approve the Seibert Anchor Cross viewing. Kyle readily agreed, saying, "I feel it will be perfectly safe staying in Randy's possession and having good police security as well. If it will help in attracting more tourism for Harlan, then I'm all for it." He then asked Fred, "Do you know what weekend it will be shown?"

Fred replied, "Still not one hundred percent, but likely will be the weekend closest to October 10th. That way we can remind folks about the *Pelle Anchor Cross* showing last October 10th, and say that this viewing will be on the anniversary of the one last year. Those that were there at the ceremony last year will remember the big explosion that occurred just as the Pelle Anchor Cross viewing started, and will realize they have another chance to view one of these historical Savior's Crosses this year, and hopefully under more peaceful conditions."

"Makes sense to me," said Kyle. "And since the viewing will take place in the memorial, it will be under better controlled conditions."

Bert then said, "Since we've got that all settled, let me update you a bit on some very interesting events of yesterday and this morning."

All looked very expectantly at Bert.

Bert said, "Kyle's already aware of this, but Randy and Raymond are not. Fred is aware of yesterday's event, but not the one that took place this morning."

Bert went on to tell Raymond, Fred, and Randy about the visit he had yesterday afternoon from Trigger Green, and then the attempt on his life this morning by Eagle Eye Looney.

After listening to all the details, Fred commented, "Well, the good thing is that we now know the hit man. I assume you're going to keep a close tab on him, and hopefully we'll be able to find out who paid him. Bert had told me about Trigger's visit yesterday, but the thing this morning comes as a real shock. Is there anything the city can do to help you Bert?"

"I think we'll have it all under control," Bert replied. "I'll let you know if I think of anything you could help with."

Randy then said, "That is a shock. But like Fred said, it is a big help to know that Eagle Eye is the man to watch."

Raymond then added, "This will be on my mind while I'm on my trip. I'll certainly keep you in my prayers, and pray that the Lord will keep you safe."

Bert then said, "Speaking of your trip that starts tomorrow, how about giving us a little update on it Raymond."

"Glad to," said Raymond. "As I've told you before, the trip is a very long one. I'm going to ride to Lexington with Randy tomorrow. My flight leaves Bluegrass Field in Lexington at 6:10 tomorrow evening, and I don't arrive in Victoria, Seychelles until 1:40 pm local time on Monday.

That works out to be about twenty hours of time in the air, but with the layovers about thirty-five hours after leaving Lexington. There's an eight-hour time difference between Lexington and Victoria, and those hours are lost on the way over. I'll certainly be exhausted after that trip. But then upon arrival I get taken to a hotel in Victoria and will get fed and have a good night's rest. The following day, Tuesday, my fellow minister, Father Elmer Schmidt from Chicago, and I will get together with our coordinator, Father Peter Alexander. He will take us on a tour of Victoria, and we will discuss details of the upcoming itinerary. After getting another good night's rest, we start on our visits to five different sites. We'll be at a plantation North of Victoria on Wednesday and Thursday. Then we go to a village in the Southern part of Mahe Island called Anse Boileau for Friday and Saturday, next to a place called Beau Villon close to Victoria for Sunday and Monday, then we travel by boat to Silhouette Island, about twenty miles Northeast of Mahe Island, for Tuesday and Wednesday, and we end up on Thursday and Friday at North Island, about seven miles North of Silhouette Island. Arrangements have been made for us to fly from North Island back to Victoria on Saturday morning, and after a briefing on Saturday we leave to fly back home on Saturday afternoon. If all goes according to plan, I should arrive back in Lexington on the following Monday. Randy has graciously agreed to pick me up and allow me to spend Monday evening with him, and then will drive me back to Harlan on Tuesday. So I'll actually be gone about seventeen days. I'm already worn out!"

Raymond continued, "At each of the five places we will visit, during the day we will go to different establishments to meet people, and to invite them to the services we will be doing each evening at a church or chapel in that area. Father Schmidt will do one service, and I will do one service at each site. It should be most interesting and rewarding."

"I hope you plan to write a book about your trip when you return," Kyle said.

"I certainly should have enough material for one," Raymond replied. "I do plan to hold at least one service at the church to give a report on the trip. I hope each of you will be able to attend."

"You can count on that, Raymond," Fred said. "We'll all be right there on the front row!"

Bert then said, "It sounds to me like everything is very well planned. I bet everything goes exactly as scheduled and you have a great seventeen days . . . but I don't envy you those long airplane trips."

"Yeah, I do dread those, but haven't figured any other way to get there," said Raymond with a grin.

Betty and Carolyn walked into the living room. Betty announced, "Folks, dinner is served. Bring your appetites and gather at the table!"

Rounds of approving nods and gestures followed as the five men stood and walked into the dining room and joined Betty and Carolyn at the dinner table.

The food looked wonderful. Pastor Bell then asked everyone to please join hands and he offered thanks to the Lord for the blessings of the day and for the food. During the course of the meal there was much small talk, and the men brought the ladies up to date on the problems Bert had encountered from Eagle Eye. Betty discussed her upcoming trip, leaving Monday for Tavares, Florida to visit with friends and relatives during the time of Raymond's absence.

After the meal, Kyle, Carolyn, Fred, and Bert all thanked the Bells for their wonderful hospitality, and wished them the very best on their trips. Randy, Raymond, and Betty then relaxed and chatted for an hour or so prior to turning in for the evening. Randy and Raymond would then be off to Lexington around noon the next day.

Chapter 18

—⁓—

Harlan, Kentucky

After a good night's rest, Randy and Raymond were treated to one of Betty's special breakfasts. Betty told Raymond this would be the last meal she prepared for him for at least seventeen days, so he better enjoy it. It was a very special breakfast, one to rival the Cracker Barrel! Eggs, bacon, sausage, ham, grits, fried potatoes, home- made biscuits, Jellies and jams, and coffee and orange juice. After the excellent meal, the three took their coffee cups to the living room and sat to allow their meal to digest and to discuss the upcoming trips.

Randy said, "Betty, I could never live in Harlan. If I did

I'd get so fat I couldn't walk from enjoying your meals! That breakfast was the best . . . thanks so much."

Raymond then said, "Honey it was very special. Thank you for doing it for us."

"Oh, you boys know how I love to cook. I'm just glad you enjoyed eating it as much as I did preparing it," Betty replied.

Randy then said, "Well Raymond, my friend, the time of departure is just about at hand. I'm not trying to rush you, but anytime you wish to hit the road we'll be off to Lexington."

Raymond replied, "Yeah, I guess the time is just about at hand. I hope I've packed everything I'm going to need. Betty helped a lot with the clothes, and I made a list of all the other stuff I needed to take. I managed to get all that into two suitcases, and I've got a carry-on as well. So as far as I know I'm good to go! We can chat a bit longer to let the food digest, and then we'll hit the road."

"I'm looking forward greatly to my trip to Florida on Monday," Betty added. "It's been a while since I've been able to visit with all my friends and relatives around Tavares. I just know that my two weeks down there will fly by and I'll not get to see everyone on my list. But I'll sure give it a good try."

Betty, Raymond, and Randy continued to chat for another

hour or so, and then Raymond and Randy loaded up the car and after ample hugs and kisses with Betty they were off.

After driving Highway 119 to Pineville, Randy turned North on 25E to head toward Corbin and Interstate 75. Randy said, "Raymond, I always think of the early pioneers traveling this route, then called the Wilderness Trail. I think often about what a hard journey it must have been for Karl and Mary Seibert back in 1798 when they passed through Cumberland Gap and then turned their wagon toward Harlan, then called Mount Pleasant.   And to think that the Savior's Cross that Reverend Seibert was wearing had a history going back to the time of Christ and was being taken into Harlan County."

Raymond replied, "It is very hard to understand the conditions then, and the situations that they had to endure. I'm just thankful that you were able to do such a great job researching those anchor crosses and to establish their origin and history. Without that we would have never understood their significance. Two scriptures always come to mind when I think about them. Hebrews 6:19 says, 'We have this hope (meaning salvation through Christ) *as an anchor of the soul, sure and steadfast'*. And then First Corinthians 1:18 says, *'For the message of the cross is foolishness to those who are perishing, but to us who are being saved it is the power of God'.* I think in those two passages the bible brings to light the significance of both the anchor and the cross, and those two are symbolized together in the beautiful Savior's Crosses."

"Thank you Raymond," Randy replied. "The Savior's Crosses are certainly very, very special. And I'm so thankful to have been a part of establishing that the Seibert and Pelle anchor crosses were two of the six that Constantine the Great made from gold traced back to having been blessed by Jesus Christ. That just makes chills run up my spine every time I think about it. And I feel so blessed to have both of the artifacts on display in the Center for Appalachian Research."

"Randy, do you think about the other four Savior's Crosses? They must be out there somewhere," said Raymond.

Randy replied, "Hardly a day goes by that I don't think of them. I've researched them, but just haven't been able to find out what happened to them. I've made contact with the Italian government and the Vatican, but without any luck. They are either lost, or they are at some location where they're not publicly known. But I'll keep trying to locate them. I'm sure each of them has quite a story, and I'd sure like to uncover it."

Raymond nodded in understanding. On they traveled

toward Lexington. They arrived around 2 pm, and went to Randy's home to relax a bit before going to Bluegrass Field. At about 4 pm they loaded up again and drove the five mile trip to the airport. Randy pulled up in front of the terminal, and the two got out of the car and unloaded Raymond's luggage from the trunk.

Randy said, "Well my friend, time to leave you. I wish you a good and safe journey. You have my phone number should you need my help on anything. God speed, and I'll see you back here in about seventeen days."

Raymond replied, "I can't thank you enough, Randy. You are a true friend indeed."

The two embraced in a big bear hug, and Raymond walked into the terminal.

Chapter 19

Harlan, Kentucky

It was Monday morning, and Judge Oakes was on the bench. After hearing a half dozen other cases, the bailiff called for Sylvester Calvin Looney to come forward. Lots of giggles could be heard in the courtroom as Deputy Kyle Potter brought Eagle Eye Looney before the bench.

Judge Oakes looked down his nose through his glasses at Kyle and Eagle Eye.

"Mr. Looney, are you not represented by counsel?" asked the judge.

Eagle Eye replied, "No your honor, I don't need no lawyer. I'll represent myself."

"Very well, Mr. Looney," said Judge Oakes. "You have been charged with the attempted murder of Harlan County Sheriff J. Bert Sterling, how do you plea?"

"Not guilty, your honor," Eagle Eye replied.

The judge then asked if Sheriff Sterling was present. Bert stood up and responded affirmatively. The judge then asked him to give his account of what happened on the previous Friday morning.

Bert began, "Your honor, I was sitting at my desk in my office around 7:20 am last Friday morning when I heard a terrible scream and lots of commotion coming from the reception room next door. I walked to my office door and opened it to see Mr. Looney standing just inside the front door with blood all over his face and a pistol lying at his feet. It was apparent to me that Preacher Puss, the office's very special cat, had just attacked Mr. Looney when he walked in with a gun in his hand. As your honor is aware, Preacher Puss has this thing about guns, and will attack anyone displaying one. It is my belief that Mr. Looney came to the department to kill me, and probably would have if not for being attacked by Preacher Puss."

Judge Oakes said, "Mr. Looney, what do you have to say for yourself?"

"Not true, your honor. Not true at all," said Eagle Eye. "I found that gun lying on the street just outside Creech Cafe just after I got out of my car Friday morning getting ready to run some errands. I felt to turn the gun in to the sheriff was the right thing to do, so I walked across the street and into the Sheriff's Department. Just as soon as I walked in the door something attacked me, and I guess from what Bert just said it was a pussy cat, but he stuck his claws in my head and I thought I was going to die. Bert then opened his door and saw me and placed me under arrest for attempted murder. It ain't right, your honor, I've been in jail for 3 days for trying to be a good citizen. I plan to get an attorney and sue the sheriff's office for false arrest and for an attack by the sheriff's pussy cat."

Judge Oakes was trying real hard to keep from laughing, but a big grin broke out on his face as he said, "Sheriff, you have any evidence that Mr. Looney was trying to kill you?"

"Only what I have told you, your honor," Bert replied.

"Then you have no evidence," said Judge Oakes. "I have no option other than to release Mr. Looney. Deputy Potter, please take Mr. Looney out of the courtroom. He is free to go."

"Thank you judge," Eagle Eye said. "I tried to tell 'em, but they wouldn't listen. You'll be hearing from my lawyer, Bert."

Kyle walked with Eagle Eye out of the courtroom and then took off his handcuffs.

"Eagle Eye, I'm going to tell you this one time and you better understand it. We have reason to believe that you have been paid to kill Bert. You tried once and failed. I'm making it my personal business to keep an eye on you, and if I see anything suspicious I'll haul you back to jail. Next time we'll have some definite evidence to put you away again for a good long time. You better think long and hard about that before you do something else stupid," Kyle said.

"Talk, talk, talk. I don't have to listen to you. I'm out of here," Eagle Eye said, and then turned and walked out of the courthouse to his car.

Thirty minutes later Eagle Eye pulled into Maggard's grocery. Deputy Potter was driving his personal unmarked car and drove on past the grocery after seeing Eagle Eye stop there. He turned around after about a quarter mile and came back and parked across the street about one hundred yards from the grocery. He was parked in a spot where he could watch Eagle Eye's car and the entire parking lot in front of the store.

Eagle Eye walked into the store.

"Eagle Eye, you're back! You stay gone for years and now

you're back after just a few days. What's going on?" said Fatso Chapel.

"I need a rifle," said Eagle Eye. "You got one?"

"Whoooa," Fatso replied. "You just bought a pistol a few days ago, and now you want a rifle?"

"None of your damn business what I need it for. Can you sell me one or not? Eagle Eye replied.

"Maybe, maybe not," Fatso said. "I'll have to check with the chief."

"Go," said Eagle Eye.

"First, do you know how to tell if an elephant is getting ready to charge?" asked Fatso.

Eagle Eye just glared at him.

"You can tell he's getting ready to charge if he pulls out his American Express card," Fatso said with a chuckle as he pushed the button to unlock Trigger's door and walked toward his office.

Fatso walked into Trigger's office.

Trigger was sitting at his desk reading a magazine. He looked up at the monitor connected to a camera in the grocery store and then at Fatso and said, "I see our dumb friend Eagle Eye is back. What's he want now?"

"Says he wants a rifle," Fatso responded.

Trigger thought about it for a minute, and then said, "Send him back here."

Fatso walked back to the check-out counter and said to Eagle Eye, "Boss says to come on back."

Fatso once again pressed the button opening the door to Trigger's office and Eagle Eye walked through.

"Our repeat customer is back," said Trigger, standing from his desk.

"Yeah, need a rifle Trigger," Eagle Eye said.

"May I ask what for?" responded Trigger

"Target practice," said Eagle Eye.

"Who's the target?" said Trigger

"No one, just target practice," said Eagle Eye.

"Gonna cost you," said Trigger. "Fifteen hundred bucks."

"Let me see what you got," said Eagle Eye.

Trigger walked over to the cabinet, opened it, and showed Eagle Eye the rifles he had.

"I'll take that Remington 700," said Eagle Eye.

"Only if you come up with fifteen hundred dollars first," said Trigger.

Eagle Eye pulled out the roll of one hundred dollar bills, and peeled out fifteen of them.

"Sure is expensive target practice," said Trigger as he pocketed the bills and handed the rifle to Eagle Eye.

"I gotta have something to hide this thing in, I can't just go carrying it out of the store," Eagle Eye said.

"Fatso'll put it in something, you take care Eagle Eye, I'd hate to see your target get the best of you," said Trigger.

Eagle Eye took the rifle, turned, and walked through the door into the grocery store.

"Fatso, Trigger said you'd put this rifle in something to hide it," Eagle Eye said.

"Yeah, I could do that," replied Fatso as he reached under the counter and got a large garbage bag and handed it to Eagle Eye.

Eagle Eye then put the rifle in the garbage bag, turned to leave the store, and said, "See you later, Fatso."

"Hey Eagle Eye, you know which elephants don't get toothaches?" said Fatso.

"The ones that use Crest," Fatso said to Eagle Eye as he slammed the door going out.

Deputy Potter saw Eagle Eye come out of the grocery

carrying a large, black garbage bag. He felt sure there was something illegal in it, but he couldn't search him without his having violated some law. Putting a garbage bag in his car didn't qualify.

Eagle Eye pulled out of the parking lot. Kyle was close behind.

Chapter 20

Victoria, Seychelles

Father Alexander was awaiting the arrival of his two ministers. He was in the baggage claim area of the Victoria Airport, and held a sign that said 'Schmidt and Bell'. He had learned that Father Schmidt had joined with Pastor Bell when both arrived at the Atlanta airport, and had traveled from there on the same flights. The final leg of their trip was a flight from Abu Dhabi to Victoria, scheduled to arrive at 1:40 pm. Father Alexander looked at his watch and saw that it was now almost 2:00 pm. He knew the flight was listed as being 'on time', so he anticipated the arrival of the two ministers any minute now. People were starting to wait by the baggage carrousel for their luggage. It was just then that Father Alexander saw two very tired looking gentlemen walking toward the carrousel and pointing toward him and his sign.

"I'm Father Peter Alexander," he said as he extended his hand.

Father Schmidt and Pastor Bell shook hands with Father Alexander and the three chatted about the trip and learned a little about each other as they waited to retrieve the luggage. They then walked to Father Alexander's car and made the trip into Victoria to their hotel. It was agreed that the two ministers should get all settled in their rooms and take a brief nap, and then they would all three meet for dinner at the hotel restaurant at 7 pm. Following dinner the two ministers would get a good night's rest to get caught up on their sleep, and then meet the following morning at 8 am in the hotel restaurant for breakfast. Father Alexander would then take them on a sightseeing tour of Victoria during the day on Tuesday, and then allow them another good night's rest before starting the short trip on Wednesday to the Faure Plantation.

The time the three had spent together on Monday afternoon and at dinner, and then all day Tuesday, served to allow them to establish a good bond. They got along famously, and when on Wednesday they began their rounds to the five sites they felt very comfortable and compatible with each other.

As they left Victoria headed for the Faure Plantation Father Alexander talked as he drove, "Gentlemen, our first stop is a very interesting one. We will begin by going to Maidive Village, located just outside the plantation. We'll be staying in a hotel there, and after getting our rooms and getting settled in, I have several places in the village I wanted you to visit. Just to get to know some of the folks, and to invite them to our services tonight and tomorrow evening. We'll spend the entire afternoon in Maidive Village, have an early dinner, and then drive the mile or so over to the Faure Plantation for the evening service at the beautiful little chapel on their grounds. The evening services begin at 7 pm, so we'll try and get there around 6 pm to meet the plantation's owner, Felix Faure, and Father Morgan, the resident priest. I really enjoyed meeting the two of them on my previous visit, and I'm sure you will find them very supportive and interesting. My understanding is that Raymond will be conducting the service tonight, and Elmer the one tomorrow evening. Is that correct?"

"That's our plan," Raymond responded. "Elmer and I have discussed the itinerary and have agreed to alternate on the services. I will take the first service at each site, and Elmer will take the second. We arrived at this arrangement using the good ole American 'toss of the coin'. Heads got the first service, tails got the second. I got heads."

The trio arrived at Maidive Village, and all went as planned there. Just before 6 pm they arrived at the Faure Plantation chapel. As they parked their car they saw Felix Faure and Father Morgan standing outside the chapel doors with beaming smiles on their faces.

After introductions were made and hugs and handshakes exchanged, the five started inside the chapel.

Felix Faure said as they entered, "Gentlemen, welcome to the Red Bones Chapel. If it meets with your schedule and approval I thought I would first give you a little history, and then Father Morgan can discuss the particulars of the services with you. We'll go in and be seated in the front of the chapel, but I did want to point out here in the vestibule the beautiful wooden 'Red Bones Anchor Cross' displayed there in the cabinet. We'll talk more about it after we're seated."

Father Schmidt walked first up to the cabinet and studied the cross, and then trailing behind him Raymond got a good look at the anchor cross.

The color drained from Raymond's face as he looked at the wooden anchor cross.

Felix Faure, who was standing beside the cabinet, then asked, "Pastor Bell, you have a strange look on your face and look quite pale, are you feeling ill?" The other three then turned to look at Raymond.

Raymond then said weakly, "No, no, I'm sorry. I feel fine. It's just that when I got a good look at that anchor cross it seemed very familiar to me. It's shaped exactly like two others that I have had the pleasure of examining recently back in Kentucky. It appears to have the precise dimensions and shape. And I have never seen similar anchor crosses. The big difference is that the ones in Kentucky were made of gold, and this one, of course, is wooden."

The color then drained from the faces of Felix Faure and Father Morgan.

"Did I say something wrong," asked Raymond as he noticed the look on their faces.

Felix replied, "After tonight's service I would like to talk further with you about this, Pastor Bell."

"Certainly," Raymond said. "I'll look forward to it."

The five of them then walked into the chapel and took seats on the front row.

Felix then stood before them and said, "As I mentioned previously, I wanted to share with you a brief history of the chapel. People will start coming in for the service in about a half hour, so I'll make my remarks short, and then let Father Morgan have time to go over the particulars for the two services. The plantation was started around 1820 by my great, great, great, great grandfather, Jean-Paul Faure. In 1855 he asked the Catholic Church to establish this chapel, which they did. In 1860 Jean-Paul Faure was horseback riding on the plantation beside the seashore, and noticed two people drifting on a wooden raft. As it turns out, these two, one called 'Red' and the other 'Bones', had been on a ship that was destroyed in a storm. Apparently they were the only survivors. They had drifted on a piece of wood from the sunken ship for 3 days before landing at the plantation. Red was wearing on a necklace the beautiful wooden anchor cross that you saw displayed in the vestibule. He attributed their survival to the power represented by the anchor cross. Jean-Paul offered the two of them jobs working on the plantation, and they accepted. After attending services in this very chapel the two accepted the Word of Christ and became devout Christians. They continued to serve on the plantation until their deaths. Then in 1925 the chapel was dedicated as the Red Bones Chapel. So now you know a bit of its history. I know time is growing short before tonight's service, so I'll let Father Morgan chat with you."

Father Morgan quickly discussed details of the upcoming two services, and then the four ministers and Felix Faure walked back to the chapel's entrance to greet those arriving for the evening service.

The chapel began to fill quickly. By 7 pm there was hardly a seat to be found. Over one hundred people were in attendance. Father Morgan greeted everyone and then offered a warm prayer. Two hymns were then sung, after which Father Morgan introduced Pastor Raymond Bell. Raymond used a few minutes to greet the attendees and to share a bit of his background. He then spent the rest of his time delivering a sermon that focused on the Love of Christ and presented the plan of salvation. As was the custom at New Hope Baptist Church in Harlan, Kentucky, at the conclusion of the sermon another hymn was sung and Raymond made an appeal for anyone attending that had not accepted Christ to come forward and receive Him. Fourteen persons did so. It was a wonderful, uplifting service, and all the ministers spent time meeting and answering questions from the attendees after the service was concluded.

About a half hour after the conclusion of the evening service all of the attendees had finally left. Only Felix Faure and the 4 ministers remained in the chapel.

Felix said, "Gentlemen, it was a beautiful, very meaningful, and fruitful service. I'm so thankful especially for the fourteen new Christians, and I'm sure that all the rest attending received a real blessing, as did I. Now for a little unfinished business. If you would be so kind as to walk with me back to the vestibule, I'd like to talk a little more about the wooden anchor cross."

All nodded in agreement, and they walked together to the back of the chapel and then into the vestibule.

Felix then said, "Pastor Bell, you told us that the shape of this anchor cross looked familiar to you, I wonder if you would care to elaborate a bit on that?"

"Certainly, I would be happy to," Raymond replied. "Due to very different circumstances, two beautiful, golden anchor crosses with shape and dimensions exactly like this wooden anchor cross found their way to my home town of Harlan, Kentucky. A very good friend of mine by the name of Dr. Randy

Peters is Director of a center at the University of Kentucky in Lexington called The Center for Appalachian Research. When the first of these golden anchor crosses turned up in Harlan about thirteen years ago, having been brought into the county originally by a settler named Seibert in 1798, I asked Dr. Peters for his help and expertise in trying to identify it. As it turns out, he was able to establish that it could be traced back to the Roman Emperor Constantine the Great, who around 325 A.D. commissioned six of the golden anchor crosses, called the Savior's Crosses, to be made from gold that was given him by Pope Sylvester I. And that gold, called St. Peter's gold, could be traced back in the church all the way to Saint Peter, after having been blessed by our Lord Jesus Christ and given to him to help start the church."

Father Morgan then said, "I think I need to sit down, lets grab some chairs!" All five pulled up chairs and sat before the cabinet housing the wooden anchor cross.

Felix Faure said, "That's just an incredible story, please continue."

Raymond continued, "Then, about a year ago one of Dr. Peters' colleagues at the University of Kentucky happened across a similar golden anchor cross in a church in Prato, Italy.

Upon learning from his colleague about it, Dr. Peters' traveled there and found that it was on loan to the church from a fellow named Domenico Pelle. Mr. Pelle owns the extensive Pelle vineyards and wine company in Prato. Dr. Peters and Mr. Pelle quickly became good friends, and traveled together back to Kentucky with the Pelle Anchor Cross to authenticate it at the Center for Appalachian Research. After it was determined beyond doubt that the Pelle and Seibert anchor crosses had been made from the same mold, Mr. Pelle decided to bring his anchor cross to Harlan to display it in a large ceremony. So that's how both of these Savior's Crosses managed to find their way to Harlan, Kentucky. They each are currently on display and are still being studied at Dr. Peters' Center for Appalachian Research in Lexington, Kentucky.

Father Morgan then said, "That is mind boggling. To think that those two artifacts were actually made from gold blessed by our Lord!"

"There's more," Raymond said. "Apparently these anchor crosses have exhibited divine power on several occasions. They both have Latin inscriptions on the face of the horizontal member of the cross that says *Pax Tecum*, meaning 'Peace be with you', and as you all are well aware, our Lord Jesus Christ was, is, and forever will be, the Prince of Peace. I won't take the time now to tell you of the many occasions where those who possessed one of the Savior's Crosses was miraculously spared from great trauma or death, but let me assure you that many such occurrences have been documented."

Felix Faure and Father Morgan looked at each other as though they had indeed seen a ghost.

Felix stood, and slowly walked around behind the cabinet that displayed the wooden anchor cross. He then with his left hand reached to the top, right side of the cabinet and slid a small piece of the wood upwards revealing a button. He pressed this button with his left forefinger and at the same time slid a panel on the back of the cabinet open. He then reached inside the cabinet and removed the anchor cross, holding it's wooden face upward in his left hand. He then walked around to the front of the cabinet and stood facing the other four, who remained seated. He then took the anchor cross in his right hand and held it vertical for all to see, and then slowly turned it to reveal it's beautiful golden back. The inscription on the horizontal member of the cross beamed brightly, **Pax Tecum**.

With the exception of Father Morgan, who already was familiar with this anchor cross, the mouths of the other three ministers dropped open and their eyes widened. Color again drained from Raymond's face. He grabbed the side of his chair to support himself.

Raymond then exclaimed, "Behold the third Savior's Cross!" Tears formed in his eyes.

Felix then said, "Raymond, what you just shared with us, before ever knowing what the back side of our anchor cross looked like, confirms in my mind one hundred percent that this is indeed one of the Savior's Crosses. It is different from the other two, in that it is laminated with the wooden side, and I don't understand that or know how it happened. But the golden side exactly matches your description of the other two. I think I would like to see if Dr. Randy Peters would agree to come here to see it and to get his opinion."

Raymond said, "That was exactly what I was thinking, Felix. I have a feeling that Randy will be on the next plane out of Lexington after I tell him what I've seen. If that is okay with you."

"Wonderful," said Felix. "I'll look forward to his arrival. Please ask him to be my guest. We have plenty of room in my Plantation House."

"I'll give him a call just as soon as I get back to my hotel room. With the eight-hour time difference I should be able to catch him in his office," Raymond replied.

Father Alexander then said, "My, my. What an evening! Talk about exceeding expectations! Fourteen saved souls and the discovery of an artifact blessed by our Lord! I don't think I'll be able to sleep tonight just trying to digest everything that happened."

Father Morgan and Felix Faure then shook hands and gave hugs to the three ministers, and said how much they would be looking forward to seeing them again on Thursday evening. The good-byes were said, and the three ministers departed to drive back to Victoria.

Upon arriving back in his hotel room, Raymond immediately dug out Randy's phone number and placed a call.

Joyce, Dr. Peter's secretary, came on the intercom and said, "Randy, you have a call on line 1 from Pastor Raymond Bell."

Randy quickly reached for his phone and said, "Joyce, by all means put him on."

Randy continued, "Raymond, is that you? I hope you're not stuck somewhere in deepest Africa and want me to come to the rescue!"

Raymond chuckled and said, "As a matter of fact, it is

something like that! How are you doing my friend?"

"Doing just great," Randy replied. "Are you actually serious about me making a social call to visit you in the Seychelles?"

"Well, it really wouldn't be a social call. More like work," replied Raymond.

"You'll have to explain that," said Randy. "And by the way, what time is it over there?"

"It's about 10 pm, so I guess it must be about coffee break time in the afternoon there in Lexington," Raymond said.

"Yeah, about 2 pm. I'm still digesting a good lunch. So, tell me all about this work call I might need to make," asked Randy.

"You are sitting down, right?" asked Raymond.

"Oh boy, why do I get the feeling the hammer's getting ready to drop?" said Randy.

"No, no. It's all good. But almost unbelievable," said Raymond.

Raymond then proceeded to give all the details about his visit to the Red Bones Chapel, and the discovery of the wooden-golden anchor cross. He could detect deep breathing and many gasps on the other end of the transatlantic phone connection.

"I've heard a lot of strange stories in my life, Raymond, but I think that one takes the cake!" exclaimed Randy. "The moment we hang up I'll be looking for an airplane ticket to Victoria. With any luck I should be able to get out of Lexington on Friday, and would then arrive in Victoria on Sunday. I really appreciate Mr. Faure agreeing to put me up at his plantation . . . that alone would probably be worth the trip. But my mind is just spinning thinking about that laminated anchor cross. Off the top of my head, I just don't have a clue what that's all about, but I'm sure there's quite a story behind it, and you can bet that I'll not leave a stone unturned until I learn everything about it."

Raymond said, "I sort of thought you might get a little excited. When Mr. Faure removed it from its display case and turned it around to reveal the golden side I thought I would faint immediately. It was breathtaking . . . truly special. A moment I'll never forget."

Randy replied, "I understand, believe me, I do understand. Now you've gotten me so excited I'll likely not be able to sleep tonight!! At any rate, I can't thank you enough for your call, and I'll not bother you upon my arrival. I'll rent a car and drive to the plantation . . . sounds like it's only maybe ten miles or so, but I'll hope we will be able to get together sometime while I'm there. It'd be a shame for two good friends to be on the same little island half way around the world and not get together for a meal!"

"We'll make it happen," said Raymond. "I'm sure I could break away long enough for you to buy me a meal."

"It would be my great pleasure," said Randy. "I'll let you get a little sleep now. I'm sure you have another very busy day tomorrow. Thanks again for everything, and we'll make contact again after I get to the Faure Plantation. Take care my friend"

"Till we meet again, my friend," said Raymond.

Chapter 21

Harlan County, Kentucky

Deputy Kyle Potter arrived in his personal car at the vantage point about one half mile from the home of Eagle Eye and his brothers. It was just about 7 am. Kyle had been tailing Eagle Eye now for several days since he got out of jail for the attempted murder of Sheriff Sterling. Kyle had learned that each day Eagle Eye usually got out of the house after his brothers had gone to work. They usually left just before 8 am each morning. As he looked using his binoculars from his parking spot pretty well concealed by trees, he became worried. This morning he didn't see Eagle Eye's twenty-year-old pick-up truck. It was usually easy to spot and follow. Twenty years ago

Kyle figured it had been a canary yellow, but it was now faded so bad you could hardly discern it's color, plus it looked like someone had taken a hammer and beat on about every square foot. But this morning, it was nowhere to be seen. Kyle had been trailing Eagle Eye each morning from 7 am until about 5 pm, at which time he switched off with Deputy Bill Black who stayed with Eagle Eye for the next four hours. By 9 pm each evening Eagle Eye was always back at his home. So from 9 o'clock each evening until 7 o'clock the next morning Eagle Eye was left unwatched. Something was wrong this morning. Kyle could feel it. He immediately started his engine and sped away headed for the Sheriff's Department.

Eagle Eye had spent another $100 to get his buddy, Badass Brown, to loan him his thirty-year-old van truck. It was an old bread truck and still had very faded signs on it that said 'Bunny Bread'. It had been modified by Badass to have windows in the side. He had used it for camping. You could stand in it. Eagle Eye told Badass that he only wanted to use it for the morning, and that he wouldn't even be driving it. He instructed Badass to drive the van at 6 am this morning and park it on Central Street directly in front of Creech Cafe. He was told to leave it there unlocked. Eagle Eye told Badass he was going to use the van as a place to work that morning doing a small repair job for Fred Knapp. Badass was told he could come and pick up the van anytime after lunch.

It was about five minutes past 7 am. Sheriff J. Bert Sterling had parked his car beside the court house, and had just walked the short distance to the entrance of the Sheriff's Department. He noticed the old 'Bunny Bread' truck parked in front of Creech Cafe, and wondered what that was all about. He was standing at the outside entrance door to the sheriff's department, reaching for his key to unlock it.

From the van's open window facing the court house there appeared a rifle barrel. Inside the van Eagle Eye was taking careful aim toward his target. He had the back of the Sheriff's head in the cross hairs of his rifle. He had been trained in all the proper techniques required of a sniper. He took a deep breath, then held it, and very slowly began to pull the trigger.

Bert had just placed the key in the lock and started to turn it when he heard the loud explosion. He immediately turned and looked in the direction of the noise, and saw that the Bunny Bread truck had smoke coming from its window. He immediately began to run toward the truck. After reaching it, he ran to its back doors and threw them open. Inside, in a cloud of smoke, Eagle Eye Looney lay prone. There was a rifle beside him with the barrel shredded open. Bert immediately recognized what had happened. Eagle Eye had tried to shoot the gun, and it had malfunctioned and the bullet had exploded in the barrel, causing the barrel metal to shred. Eagle Eye was knocked unconscious, and was bleeding heavily from his head and left arm and hand. The Sheriff reached for his cell phone and called 911. An ambulance was on the way.

Only about five minutes later the paramedics arrived and began treating Eagle Eye. Bert had tried to slow the blood loss by taking off his shirt and wrapping it tightly around the wounds. After working on him for a few minutes the paramedics told Bert that they thought everything was under control, and they were going to take him to the hospital. Bert told them to be sure a security person was posted as guard outside Eagle Eye's room, and they said it would be taken care of.

Just as the ambulance was leaving with its emergency lights flashing and its siren blasting, Deputy Kyle Potter pulled up and jumped out of his car. Bert was standing in front of Creech Cafe with blood all over his undershirt and hands.

Kyle ran up to Bert and said, "Are you okay? What happened?"

Bert grinned at Kyle and said, "What happened to my protection?"

"You must be okay if you're kidding," Kyle replied. "I bet I can guess who was in that ambulance that just left."

"If you guessed Eagle Eye Looney you guessed correctly," replied Bert.

"Boy, am I sorry. I got to his house at 7 am and saw that his car was gone and figured he likely left home early. I got here as fast as I could, but it looks like I just missed the action," Kyle said.

Bert explained, "Yeah, he tried to shoot me as I was opening up the office. I saw the old van sitting here but didn't think much of it. Just as I was opening the door I heard this loud explosion, and saw smoke coming from the van window. When I got there Eagle Eye was laying flat on the floor bleeding big time. Apparently the rifle malfunctioned. When he pulled the trigger it exploded. He was knocked out and received lots of wounds. I called 911 and used my shirt to try and slow the blood loss. The paramedics said they thought he'd make it."

"I really feel responsible, Bert. I should have been on his tail," replied Kyle.

"Hey buddy, don't feel bad. You have to sleep sometime.

It certainly was not your fault, and besides, I didn't get injured one bit . . . just lost my shirt!" Bert kidded.

"Well, I do feel bad," said Kyle. "But I'm sure thankful that you are okay. Let's get over to the office and get you cleaned up. We might even come up with another shirt for you."

Deputy Rosie Cain was just getting to the office when Bert and Kyle walked up. Rosie took one look at Bert and about fainted. She said, "Oh my Lord, Bert, are you okay?"

Bert grinned again, patted Rosie on the shoulder, and said, "I'm just fine. Let's get inside and we'll tell you all about it."

•••

Fatso walked into Trigger's office with a big grin on his face.

Trigger looked up from his desk and said, "What's the big grin about?"

Fatso replied, "I was just listening to my radio, tuned in to the news on WHLN, and they said that Eagle Eye Looney was involved in some kind of accident this morning and had been taken to the hospital in bad shape. They said he was in an old converted bread truck parked in front of Creech Cafe and some kind of explosion occurred that knocked him out and caused a lot injury to his head and left arm and hand. Care to guess what that explosion was?" And Fatso chuckled loudly.

A big grin then began to form on Trigger's face, and he said, "It sure took him long enough. I was beginning to wonder if our little trick was going to work. From what you just said it sounds like he worked something out with one of his buddies for a van to use for his sniper shot."

"You had it all figured out, Trigger," Fatso said. "When that monster pussy cat in the sheriff's office spoiled his try at Bert using our pistol, you told me you thought he'd likely show back up here looking for a rifle. And sure enough he did. But what was really cleaver of you was to only have one rifle in the cabinet that would suit Eagle Eye, and that was the Remington 700. All the others you had in there wouldn't have been suitable."

Trigger then said, "Well, that wasn't too hard to figure out. I really got mad when I heard that he had actually tried to kill Bert with that pistol he got from us. I know he told us that he intended to use it to shoot the sheriff, but I sort of thought that was just talk. We all know old Eagle Eye's big on talk, and dumb to boot. So when we learned that he actually did try to kill the sheriff, I just started planning on a way to put him out of business if he tried it again. I like Bert, I didn't want to see him killed. And since Eagle Eye was a sniper in the army, I just figured his next move would involve trying to hit him using a rifle. And I knew he didn't have one, and would likely come here to get it. That's when I arranged the rifles so that I knew he would select the Remington 700, and then I just got a big piece of bubble gum, stuck a little lead fishing sinker in it and then stuffed it down the barrel. I knew that would cause the gun to explode on him when he fired it, and I was counting on him being too dumb to check to make sure the barrel was clear. But I thought he'd try a little target practice with it before actually trying to make the hit, so I figured he'd wind up dead or injured well before now. But I guess he was even dumber than I thought, and when he tried to shoot Bert this morning it was the first time he'd tried to fire the gun. My leaded bubble gum worked like a charm. I wonder how bad off he is?"

"The radio didn't say," Fatso replied.

"I just hope he's laid up for a long time. And that'll cause him some real problems with Pretty Boy. I don't think we have to worry any more about him trying to take out the sheriff," Trigger said.

"Yeah, I feel a lot better now," replied Fatso as he turned to walk back into the grocery store.

"Hey Trigger, what did the elephant say to the maharajah?"

Silence.

"The elephant said, 'Get off my back,'" Fatso said with a chuckle as he pulled the door shut.

Chapter 22

Harlan, Kentucky

Mayor Fred Knapp was returning to Creech Cafe after having an 8 am meeting at city hall. Just as he was leaving the meeting, around 9 am, an official told him there had been a disturbance earlier that morning just outside his store. As he arrived at Creech's he noticed the old Bunny Bread van parked directly in front of his store with yellow crime scene tape wrapped around it. Fred went into his restaurant and asked his employees if they knew anything about the van. One of them told him that they had heard that it involved some kind of explosion and that Sheriff Sterling and Eagle Eye Looney were involved. They said Deputy Potter had placed the yellow tape around the van and had told them that a wrecker would be there to pick it up.

Fred immediately called Bert on his cell phone, "Hey Bert, I just got to Creech's, had an 8 o'clock meeting at city hall, and I just found out that there was some kind of explosion associated with the old Bunny Bread van in front of the store and that it involved you and Eagle Eye . . . can you fill me in?"

Bert explained what had happened to Fred, and told him that he and Kyle would be over later for coffee and they could talk more about it. Fred said, "I'll look forward to seeing you two. I'm just relieved to know that Eagle Eye was the only one hurt."

• • •

It was around 3 in the afternoon before Bert and Kyle walked into Creech Cafe.

"It's the law, it's the law," Polly greeted them.

Kyle reached up and stroked the parrot, and then the two seated themselves at a table.

Fred appeared quickly at their table, and after pouring coffee he had a seat with them and said, "Things have certainly been busy around here today. I'm sure glad the two of you got over so we can talk. I had a very interesting call this morning from Randy Peters, and I'll tell you all about that later, but first I wanted to learn a little more about the events of this morning involving ole Eagle Eye."

Bert then responded, "Well, I told you the basics on the phone earlier. Eagle Eye's in pretty bad shape. Several fragments from the exploded rifle barrel went into both his head and left arm. The report we got from the hospital said that he would be okay. They were able to remove the metal fragments. They said he'd be in the hospital for at least another week or ten days."

Fred then said, "He got what he deserved. As far as I can tell from what you told me there's just no doubt that he had aimed that rifle at you and if it hadn't exploded you likely wouldn't be sitting here. The good Lord was looking after you, Bert."

"Amen to that," Bert replied. "And I've got no idea what caused the rifle to malfunction. I see they've hauled the van away. I asked the state police to go over everything inside, including the rifle. Maybe they can come up with something."

Fred laughed, and said, "Yeah, the wrecker got here around noon to get it. Badass Brown arrived at the same time.

Apparently it was his van, and he really got upset when he was told it was crime evidence and that it was being hauled away for investigation. Badass started cussing, stomping, threatening to sue, and turned red in the face, but they just politely hauled the van off and left him standing there. It was really comical."

Fred then asked, "Is Eagle Eye under arrest?"

Kyle replied, "He is. And the hospital has been instructed to call me just as soon as the doctors say he can be released. I'll go get him and haul him to jail. Unfortunately, Judge Oakes will likely release him again because we really don't have any evidence that he tried to kill Bert, but at least we can cause him some trouble and hold him until his court appearance. There's absolutely no doubt that this was his second attempt to shoot Bert, and when he's released he very well might try a third time."

Kyle continued, "I really felt bad that I wasn't there to stop him from trying to hit Bert, but as you said, Fred, the good Lord looked after him. One additional bit of information is that just after Judge Oakes released Eagle Eye after the Preacher Puss incident, I followed him to Maggard's grocery. He went in and after a short time came out carrying a garbage bag big enough to have a rifle in it. Trigger Green might be able to shed a little light on all this. Bert's already said he plans to give him a visit."

"Well, as they say, all's well that ends well," Fred said. "And I just hope that this is the last of Eagle Eye's assassination attempts."

"I'll vote for that," Bert replied. "He just might get lucky!"

"Okay," Fred said, "So now let me tell you about my phone call from Randy Peters this morning. He called to say he would be leaving tomorrow to fly to Victoria, Seychelles!"

Bert and Kyle got concerned looks on their faces. Kyle then said, "Is everything okay with Raymond?"

Fred responded, "Raymond's fine. Matter of fact, from what Randy said, he is having a great trip. But you're not going to believe what he turned up. In a small chapel in the northern part of Mahe island Raymond apparently found another of the Savior's Crosses!"

Bert and Kyle got astonished looks on their faces. Their mouths dropped open.

Bert said, "No way . . . you pulling our legs, Fred?"

"It's the gospel. Just reporting exactly what Randy told me. There's one big difference with this one compared to the Seibert and Pelle anchor crosses. This one has the usual golden anchor cross with the ***Pax Tecum*** inscription on one side, but laminated to it on the other side is a beautiful wooden anchor cross of the exact same size and shape."

"That is unusual, and very interesting," Kyle said. "I'd like to have seen Randy's reaction when Raymond reported his find."

"Yeah," Fred replied. "Me, too. He just got the call from Raymond yesterday, Wednesday, and tomorrow he's on his way to the Seychelles.....should arrive there on Sunday. So I'm sure he's very excited. I'll sure be anxious to learn what he finds out. He's been invited to be the house guest of the owner of a large plantation where the chapel is located. It should be interesting."

Bert and Kyle then stood and started to leave when Fred said, "You've got to let me tell you one quick story before you get back to work."

Bert and Kyle grinned, and Bert said, "Shoot. We need to leave on a cheerful note."

"See that picture up there of the church organist?" Fred asked as he pointed to a photograph posted on the wall. "That picture was taken at an old country church up toward Lynch, about 30 miles from here. The church had a visiting clergyman, and the organist wanted to make a good impression. So the organist wrote a note to the old sexton who had been a little slack in pumping enough air for the organ, and handed it to him just as the service was getting ready to begin. The sexton thought the note was intended for the visiting clergy, and passed it on to him. He opened the note and read, 'Keep blowing away until I give the signal to stop.'"

"Another good one, Fred. That'll keep us in a good mood for the rest of the day," Bert said as the two headed for the door with grins on their faces.

Chapter 23

Victoria, Seychelles

Randy was tired, very tired. It was Sunday afternoon and his plane had just landed in Victoria, almost thirty-six hours after he left Lexington. He had picked up his luggage, rented a car, and had driven to the Faure Plantation, following directions that Raymond had given him. Tired as he was, when he saw the beautiful plantation home of Felix Faure his spirits rose. He parked in front, walked to the door, and pressed the door bell.

The door opened and a distinguished looking gentleman with a big smile on his face offered his hand and said, "Welcome to the Faure Plantation. You must be Dr. Randy Peters. I'm Felix Faure, please do come in."

Randy shook hands with Felix and said, "Mr. Faure, it is a great pleasure to be here. You have a fabulous home. It reminds me of some of the beautiful Bluegrass estates around Lexington."

Felix replied, "Please call me Felix. The plantation and home have been in my family for generations. Let's go into my study and chat for just a few moments, and then I'll let you get some greatly needed rest. I trust your trip went well.

"Absolutely! It was the longest trip I've taken. I feel like my clothes are grafted to my skin!"

After reaching the study Felix said, "Please be seated, and allow me to serve you a cold glass of tea."

Randy replied, "That would be great. I ate a meal at the airport, but cold tea sounds wonderful."

Felix poured them both a tall glass of cold, sweet tea.

Felix then said, "My wife Gloria and my four children are in Victoria today, but you'll have a chance to meet them tomorrow. I know the next thing you need is about eighteen hours of sleep. Tomorrow morning, after breakfast, we'll head over to the chapel to see the anchor cross. I've got to tell you that I was just astounded to hear from Pastor Bell a bit about the history of the two anchor crosses that you now possess in your center, and from their description I feel sure the one in the chapel is also one of the Savior's Crosses. But it is a bit different from the others in that it has gold on one side and wood on the other."

Randy said, "Yes, I can't wait to see it. I've done nothing but think about it since Raymond Bell called and described it."

The two chatted for a few more minutes, and then Randy was shown to his bedroom and retired for a good long rest.

•••

"Welcome to Red Bones Chapel," Felix said to Randy. After an astoundingly good night's rest, Randy had met Felix's wife Gloria and their two sons and two daughters, and enjoyed talking with them over a delightful breakfast. Felix had then taken Randy on a tour of his plantation before winding up at the chapel. The two stood at the outside entrance steps.

"It is a beautiful structure," Randy said. "And if I recall correctly you said it was built in 1855 by your ancestor Jean-Paul Faure."

Felix replied, "That's correct. Everyone just called it 'The Chapel' up until 1925 when it was officially named the Red Bones Chapel in honor of the two called 'Red' and 'Bones' that drifted ashore here in 1860 after their ship struck a reef and sank. As I'm sure Pastor Bell told you, Red was wearing the anchor cross and credited the power associated with it to their survival. And it's that very same anchor cross that we're getting ready to see here in the vestibule of the chapel."

They walked to the entrance door and Felix unlocked it and they entered. Sunlight was coming brightly through the large windows and fell on the anchor cross in the display cabinet. Randy walked quickly to it and looked in awe.

After about a minute Randy said, "It looks exactly like the two I have at the center, except it is wooden. The craftsman that carved it was certainly extremely gifted. It is exquisite."

Felix then walked to the rear of the display cabinet and used his left hand to raise the slot in the cabinet's upper right side to reveal the button. He then pressed the button and with his right hand slid the panel in the cabinet's back side open. He reached in and removed the anchor cross and walked back around to the front of the cabinet holding the anchor cross horizontally with its wooden side facing upward. He then said,

"Why don't we walk into the chapel and have a seat. You can examine the anchor cross and we can discuss it."

After the two were seated Felix held the anchor cross vertically and rotated it 360 degrees. When Randy saw the beautiful golden side he said, "Felix, that certainly is one of the Savior's Crosses. All the details of the golden side appear to exactly match those of the Seibert and Pelle Crosses. The bonding of the wooden side to the golden side is flawless. It's beauty is beyond description."

Felix answered, "Randy, I think it's time I shared a little more of its history with you. My ancestor, Jean-Paul Faure, kept a diary. He recorded in his diary details about his conversations with Red and Bones. He was very interested to find out the origin of the anchor cross. As it turns out, the ship that Red and Bones crewed on apparently belonged to a group of thieves. The two didn't know that when they signed on, but discovered it in talking with others of the crew and overhearing some conversations from its leaders. What they gathered had happened was that the leaders, and there were about six of them, had recruited about a dozen more men and they all went on a expedition through what was then Palestine raiding temples and any other locations where they thought items of great value could be found. Those raids went on for several months. When concluded, the bandits wound up back at the Jordanian seaport of Aqaba, where they had a ship called the *Aqaba Maiden*. It was at that time that Red and Bones were recruited along with about ten others to serve as crew. The two of them had experience on fishing boats, and they were desperate for work. The diary indicated that when the one-hundred-foot-long ship left the port it had a total of about thirty persons on board. The ship was bound for the port at Durban in South Africa, where the leaders had buyers for all their stolen goods. After leaving Aqaba they sailed South down the Sea of Aqaba to the Red Sea, then to the Indian Ocean headed toward Durban. After about two weeks they encountered a terrible storm that drove their ship onto a reef. Red and Bones were on the deck, and when the ship started to sink the bow raised up at a steep angle that caused them and a lot of the cargo to shift toward the stern. Many of the cargo boxes broke open as they slammed into the stern rail. Red said he saw the beautiful anchor cross laying at his feet and grabbed it just as he and Bones jumped overboard as the ship was going down. He placed the anchor cross around his neck using the necklace attached to it, and then they found a large piece of wood and climbed aboard it. They drifted for 3 days before coming ashore at the Faure Plantation. When questioned they said they had not seen any other survivors. Red told Jean-Paul that the entire time they were adrift he had a strange feeling that they would remain safe and would survive. He also said that the anchor cross he was wearing felt warm, and that gave him comfort as well. He always attributed their survival to a divine power represented by the anchor cross."

Randy then said, "Everything you have said about that anchor cross agrees fully with my findings in researching the Seibert and Pelle Crosses. They too were each reported to represent a divine power that somehow was associated with the crosses becoming heated."

Felix continued, "Red told Jean-Paul that he knew the anchor cross was very valuable, since it contained so much gold, but that he also knew it had been stolen. But, of course, he did not know exactly from where it was stolen. He gave the anchor cross to Jean-Paul and asked that it be displayed in the chapel. Jean-Paul accepted it, and the display cabinet was made, and it's been displayed here ever since. But starting with Jean-Paul, all my forefathers were greatly bothered by the fact that the anchor cross had been stolen. No one, myself included, had any idea how to try and find its rightful owner. We only know that it likely came from somewhere in the area that is now Israel. Of course I now know the origin of the golden anchor cross portion of the artifact, but the mystery of the wooden portion remains. My instinct tells me that wherever it was stolen from in Israel would likely be the key to unlocking that mystery. Randy, I'm hoping that you'll be able to find out."

"I have been focused on the Savior's Crosses now for about thirteen years," Randy said. "Fortunately, my center has been well endowed and able to support my continued research. I'll certainly make every effort to get additional information on your anchor cross. I do agree with what you said. I too think that Israel likely is where the wooden portion was added to the golden anchor cross, and when I get back home I'll start trying to locate something from there."

Felix then handed the anchor cross to Randy. He took it, and slowly examined both sides and the edges. His eyes started to water as he studied it. Finally he said, "Felix, if this anchor cross could talk, I know it would have a story to tell that would blow our minds."

Felix responded, "Without doubt. So now I want to tell you exactly what I would like to do with the anchor cross. As soon as I heard from Raymond about your involvement with the other two Savior's Crosses I knew I wanted you to take possession of this one and try to establish as much information about it as possible. I did want to wait until I met you to make sure that I felt comfortable in parting with it. Now we've met, and I feel extremely comfortable to let you take it back to your center for study. One problem in doing that is the void that it would leave here in the chapel. To solve that problem I had this wooden anchor cross constructed."

Felix reached into his pocket and withdrew a near replica of the wooden anchor cross. He offered it to Randy, who took and examined it.

Randy said, "It certainly looks like the original. It has the exact same shape and dimensions, and the wood seems to closely match. I must admit, however, that I think the original far exceeds it in beauty. It's hard to say exactly why that is."

"I agree," said Felix. "But I do think the copy is close enough that if I put it in the display cabinet people likely would not notice the difference. I think it would pass inspection. But I would not want to deceive people. So I've also had another plaque made that is identical in every respect to the one currently on the cabinet except it reads in part, '**This beautiful**

anchor cross is similar to the one brought ashore . . . ' rather than what the current one says, **'This beautiful anchor cross was brought ashore . . .** '. And I'll ask Father Morgan to make an announcement on Sunday explaining what has happened to the original. Also, my guess is that the local media will pick up on this story and spread the news. Does that sound okay to you?"

Randy said, "Felix, I'm truly honored that you would entrust me with this priceless artifact. I can assure you I'll do everything in my power to establish its history, and will guard it with my life. It will certainly draw a vast amount of interest, and I'm sure the media will focus on it immediately. Just as the other two anchor crosses at my center are owned by Kyle Potter and Domenico Pelle, you will retain ownership of this one. But having it at the center will not only allow the public and media to view it, but it will greatly enhance my ability to study and research it. Words just cannot convey my appreciation to you for allowing me this opportunity."

Felix answered, "You could not be more welcome, my friend. My forefathers and I have been greatly troubled by the fact that the anchor cross was stolen. I now feel that somehow that dark side of its history will be resolved. You are truly a

God-send. I feel totally comfortable with our arrangement. Please do let me say, however, that in the not too distant future you are likely to see me in Lexington. I certainly would like to come and visit with you to see your center and the other two Savior's Crosses, and to see Kentucky. I hear there is much more to Kentucky than just basketball!"

"There is indeed! And I'd just love to show-off Kentucky to you. My humble home in Lexington is certainly not in the same class as your Plantation House, but I would insist you to stay with me during your visit. One of the places you would have to see is Harlan. In addition to the town and county, I have several dear friends there that I know you would enjoy meeting, and, of course, Pastor Raymond Bell lives there. So you already know one person!"

"Sounds like a plan to me," Felix said. "Pastor Bell is truly amazing. I enjoyed so much meeting and talking with him. If it had not been for his visit here to this chapel the identity of this anchor cross might never have been made. I'll certainly be looking forward to seeing him again and sharing time with him in Harlan."

"Speaking of Raymond, we're all set to have dinner tonight in Victoria. My flight back leaves out later tonight so after dinner I'll head for the airport and be off on another 36 hour trip!"

Felix took the necklace of the anchor cross, placed it around Randy's neck, and said, "Wear it home . . . it'll keep you safe."

Randy looked down at the anchor cross and said, "Not a doubt in my mind about that, my friend."

Felix then placed the replica anchor cross in the display cabinet, and the two departed the Red Bones Chapel headed for the Faure Plantation house.

•••

After many handshakes and hugs, Randy drove away from the plantation house with Felix and his entire family waving from their massive front porch. The sadness of leaving was lessened by knowing that he would see Felix again in Kentucky and also by the wonderful feeling of the anchor cross hanging on the necklace about his neck. It had indeed been a good and worthwhile trip, and he looked forward with great anticipation to seeing Raymond Bell and having dinner with him.

The drive to Victoria took only about forty-five minutes. Felix had recommended a restaurant located close to the airport in Victoria, and as he pulled into the parking lot he saw Raymond sitting on a bench just outside the restaurant entrance. He honked his horn, waved, and then parked and walked quickly to Raymond. The two embraced.

Raymond then said, "It's about time! I'm getting hungry!"

Randy grinned and replied, "Me too, let's eat!"

They walked into the restaurant and were seated.

"I can't begin to tell you how glad I am to see you," Randy said. "I was afraid your hectic schedule might not allow for our getting together. How did you manage it?"

"Fortunately today I was in a village called Beau Villon, only about five miles west from here. Father Schmidt was already scheduled to conduct the service there this evening. I had conducted the one last night. So I begged off for the evening to meet and have dinner with my dear friend. I just wouldn't for the world have missed seeing you. I want to hear all about your visit with the Faures, and what you thought about their anchor cross," Raymond said.

Randy reached down under his buttoned up sport coat and pulled out the anchor cross, careful to display the wooden side so that anyone in the restaurant might not see all the gold on the other side.

Raymond's eyes appeared about to pop out of their sockets, and he exclaimed, "My Lord. I cannot believe it. You and Felix certainly must have gotten along famously."

"We did indeed," Randy replied. "We had a wonderful time together. Their plantation home was just super, and his family was most delightful. I got a really good night's rest, and then we took a little tour of the plantation before getting to the chapel this morning. He gave me a good history of the anchor cross, including one thing that I think you don't know. The anchor cross was actually stolen by a bunch of thieves and carried aboard the ship on which Red and Bones crewed. So Felix and his forefathers had always felt badly that they knew the artifact was stolen but could not determine from whom. So Felix decided that I could possibly help establish its history, and maybe even find out its true owner, and he decided to allow me to take it back to the center for study. He also said that he plans a trip to Kentucky in the near future, and wanted to come to Harlan. So we certainly have not seen the last of him."

"Hey, that's good news," Raymond said. "Betty can whip up a good ole Kentucky meal for him."

The two friends continued with their meal and chatting for another two hours.

"Well, my friend, the ole bird is awaiting my arrival. I guess I'd better get underway to check in my rental and to get all checked in for my flight. Just think, in about 36 more hours I'll be back in Lexington," Randy said with a chuckle.

The two walked outside the restaurant.

Raymond said, "I have no doubt whatsoever about your safety on the return flight. Just make sure you keep that anchor cross around your neck."

Randy laughed and said, "You can count on that . . . I'll even try and sleep with it on. The next time we see each other will likely be at Bluegrass Field next Monday. That's only a week from now. I hope you continue to have great success with your visits, and do take care."

Raymond responded, "Thanks Randy, Pax Tecum!"

The two friends then shook hands, hugged, and went their separate ways.

Chapter 24

Harlan County, Kentucky

Fatso Chapel looked up as Sheriff J. Bert Sterling entered Maggard's Grocery.

"Morning Sheriff," Fatso said. "This a personal or business call?"

"Hey Fatso," Bert replied. "Strictly business. I need to talk with Trigger."

"I can arrange that," replied Fatso. "But first, what did Tarzan say when he saw elephants coming over the hill?"

Bert just stared at Fatso.

"Tarzan said, 'Here come elephants over the hill'!" Fatso said as he pressed the button opening Trigger's door.

Bert walked into Trigger's office. Trigger looked up from his desk and said, "Hey Bert, how can I be of assistance?"

Bert pulled up a chair and had a seat in front of Trigger's desk and said, "Morning Trigger, I won't be long. Just wanted to discuss a little matter with you. Of course you really don't have to talk to me, but I thought I'd give it a shot anyway."

Trigger replied, "I'll certainly talk with you about anything I can. Certain things are off limits for me, and I'm sure you understand that. So, what's on your mind?"

"Eagle Eye Looney," Bert replied. "He's made two attempts now to take me out, and I'm getting a bit tired of it. Dumb as he is, he could get lucky. I'd really like to make sure he doesn't try number three."

"I can understand that," replied Trigger. "But how can I do anything to control Eagle Eye? As a matter of fact, I'd heard that he was in the hospital in pretty bad shape. I don't think it likely he'll be causing you any trouble in the near future."

Bert said, "It's not the near future I'm concerned about. The hospital says he'll pull through and be out in maybe a little over a week. We've got him under arrest for the last attempt, but we don't have any evidence that will stand up in court. Judge Oakes will put him on the street as soon as he appears before him. That's what I'm concerned about."

"Still don't see what I can do to help you, sheriff," Trigger said. "Did you have something in mind?"

Bert said, "We both know that Eagle Eye's not allowed by law to have any firearms. And most of the people in the county know he's too foolish to have any, so it's about impossible for him to get guns either legally or illegally. I don't know where he got the pistol he used when he tried to take me out in my office, and luckily for me Preacher Puss saved me. And I don't know where he got the rifle that he had in the bread truck. But a little bird told me one time that you sometimes sell guns here at Maggard's Grocery. Any truth to that?"

"Now sheriff, you don't really expect a straight answer to that do you?" Trigger replied. "A person could get in trouble admitting to something like that to the law . . . you understand?"

"Before he came at me with the pistol you had given me a warning that there was a contract out for me, but we had no idea who had been hired. So after Judge Oakes released him Deputy Potter started tailing him. As soon as he left the courthouse he headed straight for Maggard's Grocery. Kyle saw him leave the grocery with a large garbage bag big enough to hold a rifle. You remember anything about that?"

Trigger scratched his head and thought for a minute, then said, "I guess he was hungry and came here for some groceries, Bert."

"I do think he was hungry, but not for food. I think he was hungry to get a rifle and use his sniper expertise to do me in," Bert responded.

Bert continued, "Let me just tell you what I think might have happened. I think he came here and asked you to buy a rifle. I think you sold him one, but either by mistake or by plan the rifle had something wrong with it. Since I believe you knew that Eagle Eye had been contracted to kill me, as demonstrated by your warning visit to me, I think when he came back and bought that rifle you felt he might get lucky and take me out. My gut feeling is that you didn't want him to do that and either sold him a faulty rifle or did something to the gun that caused it to explode when he tried to fire it. If my gut feeling is correct, I owe you for saving my life."

Bert stopped talking and just looked at Trigger straight in his eyes.

Trigger started to smile and said, "You a pretty smart fellow, Bert. Course I can't confirm what you say, but it does make perfect sense to me," and his smile got much larger.

"That's all I needed to hear, Trigger," Bert said. He then stood up and extended his hand to Trigger. They shook hands vigorously.

Trigger then said, "He won't come back to me for his next weapon. He'll either locate one somewhere else or maybe try and make something. He's dangerous Bert. I would advise you to keep close tabs on him when he gets released. I really don't want to see you get hurt."

Bert turned to leave, and looked over his shoulder and said, "I really do appreciate that Trigger, and I want you to know that. Thanks!"

As the sheriff was approaching the front door to the grocery store he heard Fatso say, "Hope your meeting went well, sheriff. You know why elephants have wrinkled knees?"

The door opened and closed.

"Elephants got wrinkled knees from playing marbles," Fatso said to himself, and then grinned.

•••

Bert walked into the Sheriff's Department, reached up and gave Preacher Puss a gentle pet, and then noticed Mayor Knapp and Deputy Kyle Potter sitting together behind the reception counter.

Bert said, "Hey guys, where's Rosie?"

Kyle responded, "She ran out on an errand, should be back shortly. Fred just came over to give me a little news."

The sheriff said, "Oh, good news I hope?"

"Yes," replied Kyle, "I'll let him tell you about it."

Bert walked behind the counter, pulled up a chair and sat.

Fred said, "I got a phone call from Randy. He was on his way back home and called during one of his layovers. I guess he's got one of those satellite phones. Anyway, he was calling to alert me that he had a very good visit with the plantation owner that had the new Savior's Cross, and that the owner had agreed to let Randy bring it back with him to display and study at his center. He said he'd tell us all about that when he got back, but he wanted me to know that since this was a new Savior's Cross we might want to consider displaying it in Harlan in our October ceremony at the memorial rather than the Seibert Cross. He thought that by then it might be heavily in the news and would perhaps draw a larger crowd. I told him that made a lot of sense to me, and depending on what he discovered about the new anchor cross we might well want to do that. He said to tell everyone 'hi', and that he was looking forward to getting back to Lexington. He said he was scheduled to arrive home around 1 am on Wednesday morning . . . that's tomorrow."

Bert said, "Indeed that is good news. I'm sure he's anxious to get back home and to start trying to discover the history of that new anchor cross. That whole thing is very exciting."

Kyle then said, "So I understand from Rosie that you went to have a chat with our friend Trigger Green. Did you uncover anything?"

"We had a nice chat," Bert replied. "As you would know, he was extremely careful not to say anything that could be held against him, but I left with a clear understanding that he or Fatso had definitely done something to Eagle Eye's rifle that caused it to malfunction and explode. He indicated that he didn't want to see me get hurt, and didn't confirm or deny that he sold Eagle Eye the rifle, but from our conversation I feel confident he did. I owe him big time for that. He also told me to really watch my back after Eagle Eye got back on the street. He said he didn't think he would come to him again to get a gun, and he thought he would either try to locate one elsewhere or try something different to fulfill the contract on me."

Fred said, "Trigger really is a crook, as everyone in Harlan

County knows, but he does have a good heart. That information is certainly good to know."

The three stood up just as Rosie walked in the front door. She looked at the three standing behind the counter and said with a grin, "Well, well, it looks like it takes three men to do my job."

"Looks can be deceiving," said Kyle. "What'd you have in those bags?"

Rosie reached into one and pulled out a bag of *Whisker Lickins* and said, "Ole Preacher Puss was running low on supplies, so I picked up those, and then needed some other stuff for the office."

Rosie then opened the *Whisker Lickins* and pulled out four or five of the treats and laid them on Preacher Puss's shelf. The cat immediately started swishing her tail and quickly gobbled the treats. When finished she lay back down and closed her eyes with a contented look on her face. Rosie reached up and gave her several gentle strokes.

The men walked from behind the reception counter.

Fred said, "Well, got to get back to Creechs. Y'all come over for coffee anytime."

"We will," Bert, Kyle, and Rosie said in unison as Fred left.

Chapter 25

Lexington, Kentucky

It was Wednesday morning, 1 am. Randy had a very long and tiring thirty-six-hour plane trip from Victoria, Seychelles, but had arrived safely at Blue Grass Field exactly on schedule. He then drove to his home and slept soundly for about fourteen hours, after which he got up, showered, and prepared a good "breakfast for dinner" meal. He watched the news from 6 to 7 pm, and then gathered his briefcase and headed for the office. He felt very refreshed, and knew that at this hour his office would be quiet and he could get lots of work done.

He first went through his mail, then his email, and read all the university correspondence he had received from his secretary, Joyce, and from colleagues. After about an hour he was satisfied that he was reasonably caught-up on everything, and then opened his briefcase and removed the anchor cross. He just sat in his chair holding and turning it for several minutes. It's beauty was beyond description! And the fact that it had the wooden back side was especially interesting to Randy. What was it, and what did it signify? There was no doubt in his mind that the golden side was definitely one of the Savior's Anchor Crosses. It was exactly identical to the Seibert and Pelle anchor crosses in his Center, and he had traced both of them back to being formed by Constantine around 325 A.D. using gold acquired from Pope Sylvester I that had originally been blessed by Jesus Christ and given to Peter to help start the church. But with this new Savior's Cross there was a mystery . . . why was a beautiful wooden anchor cross laminated to the back of the Savior's cross? This was the question that Randy had constantly thought about on his trip back home. But he had no answer.

He did, however, have a clue. Felix Faure had told Randy that the diary of Jean-Paul Faure indicated that Red had told him that the anchor cross was part of the stolen goods taken during a plundering trip made by the leaders of the ship that he and Bones crewed on. Since the ship left from the seaport of Aqaba, Randy knew that the robbers likely stole all their goods somewhere within a reasonable distance of the seaport. The seaport of Aqaba is located at the Southern tip of Jordan, and today is adjacent to Elat, the Southernmost city in Israel. In 1870, at the time of the plundering trip, Randy thought that the area around Jerusalem, about 80 miles North of Elat, would probably have been the most likely region for finding such valuables. So he thought that his research would start there. He would assume that by some means one of the Savior's Crosses had found its way from Rome to Jerusalem, and then been modified for some reason with the addition of the wooden back side. Further, it seemed to him logical that this would have taken place sometime during Constantine's rule, likely between about 325 to 337 A.D. Randy's previous research had established that the Anchor Crosses had been made by Constantine around 325 A.D., and he died twelve years later. At least this seemed like a good place to start, assuming: (1) the Savior's Cross was taken to the area of Jerusalem sometime between 325 and 337 A.D., and (2) that sometime after that the wooden back side was formed to it.

Randy got on his computer and began his search. After

several hours of unsuccessful efforts, he thought he would look at one of the most famous sites in Jerusalem, the Church of the Holy Sepulchre. It was at this site where Constantine and his mother, Helena, thought Christ was crucified, and thus erected the church. Over the years many objects of value were on display there. During the period of interest Randy discovered that the Bishop of Jerusalem was named Macarius, and that he accompanied Helena in her successful search for the True Cross. And then it was as though a light came on to Randy. Helena would certainly have known about and had access to the Savior's Crosses, and when she found the True Cross she directed that pieces of it be removed and taken back to Rome to be displayed in the palace's private chapel. Randy felt certain that he had discovered the two main pieces of the puzzle, the Savior's Cross and wood worthy to be bound to it.

Randy was very excited about the information he had turned up. He felt sure that there was a connection between Helena's visit to Jerusalem and the anchor cross. He also had the feeling that the Bishop of Jerusalem, Macarius, was involved. He spent several hours researching both Helena and Macarius, and then realized that his eyes were getting very heavy. He looked at his watch and saw that it was almost 3 am on Thursday morning.

He had to head home and get some sleep. Joyce and the rest of his staff were expecting him in the office at 8 am, and that was just about five hours off!

He placed the new anchor cross in his personal wall safe, locked up the office, and then drove to his home. On the way he thought about how fortunate things were going. He just knew that he had established enough information to define the new anchor cross. He would get some rest and then when he got back in the office in a few hours would try and piece everything together.

•••

He looked at the clock beside his bed and it informed him it was 7:45 am! He jumped out of bed and headed to the bathroom. After a quick shower he got dressed and grabbed a banana on the way out the door. It was now 8:10 am, his cell phone would be ringing shortly with Joyce wanting to know his whereabouts! Just after getting his car underway his cell rang. He explained to Joyce that he should be at the office in about fifteen minutes.

"Sorry I'm running a bit late," Randy said as he entered the door to his Center. "I stayed up a bit late last night researching the new Anchor Cross and overslept."

Joyce replied, "Excuses, excuses, excuses. It is good to see you Dr. Peters, and to know you made your long journey without problems. It's especially exciting that you were able to bring the new Anchor Cross back with you. I hope you'll have a special showing for me and the other Center staff. We're all dying to see it!"

"You bet I will," Randy replied. "I'll have everyone in sometime this afternoon to gawk at it, and I want to call a press conference for tomorrow at 3 pm to show and tell with all the media. If you would, please get a press release out to all the media announcing that the Center has acquired another Anchor Cross and will give all the details at the press conference."

"Will do, boss," Joyce replied. "Bet we have a good response!"

"Likely," Randy replied. "And they certainly won't be disappointed!"

He then walked into his office and closed the door. He walked to his wall safe, dialed the combination, and opened it. He carefully extracted the Anchor Cross, and carried it with him to his desk. He laid it on his desk and sat. He once again just looked at the artifact and thought for several minutes about its mysterious and wonderful history. How blessed he felt to have it in his possession. He looked forward greatly to sharing his knowledge about it with his Center colleagues this afternoon and with the media at the press conference tomorrow.

He then started to piece together all the information that he had unveiled during his research last night. First of all, it had become clear that Constantine's mother, Helena, had indeed made a trip to Jerusalem in 326 A.D. She had been very old at the time, almost 80, but would not be denied the chance to look for the True Cross. Randy felt certain that she either took Constantine's Anchor Cross or one of the others given to the Pope with her on the journey, but had no way of knowing which. Then he had found out from reading several accounts written into the record by Bishop Marcarius that Helena had presented the Bishop with a beautiful golden anchor cross that had joined to its back side a wooden replica that had been carved from wood removed from the True Cross. It was recorded that Helena presented this Anchor Cross to Bishop Marcarius with instructions for it to be permanently displayed in the Church of the Holy Sepulchre. Furthermore, Bishop Marcarius put in the record that the name of the artifact would be the Helena

Anchor Cross. There was just no doubt at all in Randy's mind, this Anchor Cross that now lay before him was the same one. He felt weak! Gold blessed by the Lord joined together with wood from the cross upon which he was crucified and died for the sins of the world. Just beyond description. He looked forward with great anticipation to sharing his discovery.

•••

It was a few minutes before 3 pm on Friday afternoon. The conference room in the Center for Appalachian Research was filling with media. Randy had met with all his staff on Thursday afternoon and briefed them on the history and his research findings regarding the Helena Anchor Cross, and he allowed each of them to hold and examine it. They each found it as astounding as did Randy. He then gave each of them related assignments to pursue.

Randy stood at the door to the conference room and greeted each media person as he or she arrived. There were representatives from the Louisville television stations and **The Courier Journal** newspaper. From Lexington there was a reporter from **the Lexington Herald-Leader** newspaper and the three commercial television stations. There were about half a dozen reporters from smaller town newspapers around Central Kentucky, and one representative from Kentucky Educational Television. Just when Randy thought about everyone had arrived that might be coming, in walked *Harlan Daily Enterprise* reporter A.J. Sampson along with Lexington Television station WKYT reporter Barbara Clark. Both Sampson and Clark were natives of Harlan and had been chatting together outside the conference room before the press conference got underway. Randy shook hands and greeted both reporters, and then asked them to please have a seat.

The conference room was set up to accommodate the press conference. Room was provided at the back for tripods and cameras, and in front of them there were three rows of seats for the reporters. Randy walked behind the large table in the front of the room.

"Good afternoon my friends," he said. "I appreciate your cooperation by taking the time to attend my press conference. I think when we conclude you'll agree it was time well spent. So let's get right to it."

He reached down to a locked cabinet below the table, opened the door, and extracted the beautiful Anchor Cross.

He placed it directly in front of him on the table and with a giant smile said, "Ladies and gentlemen of the press, I would like to introduce you to the Helena Anchor Cross!"

The next five minutes were first filled with gasps and murmurs exclaiming how beautiful it was, and then the sound of cameras rolling and shutter's clicking. It seemed a virtual lightening storm with all the camera flash units discharging. Finally things quieted.

Randy then started with the known history of the Helena Anchor Cross from the time it came ashore at the Faure Plantation on Mahe Island in 1860 to concluding with his bringing it to Kentucky just two days ago. Next he told them his research findings, about the trip made by Helena to Jerusalem in 326 A.D. and then about Bishop Marcarius's recorded accounts. He then put everything together as he envisioned it had happened. When finished, he took questions from the reporters for the next forty-five minutes. All the reporters then rushed out of the conference room with big grins on their faces as they scurried to get the story out as quickly as possible.

Randy was left standing behind the table looking at a totally empty room. He gathered the Helena Anchor Cross and walked to his office. He knew that the world would soon know that another of the Savior's Crosses had been found. He also knew he had some very busy days ahead.

Chapter 26

Harlan, Kentucky

"Judge Oakes, I can't believe I've been charged with attempted murder again! My good friend Badass Brown had been driving his old bread truck down town and it started to act up. He pulled it into a parking place in front of Creech Cafe and called me to come look at it. Old Badass don't know much about engines. Badass had to leave, but when I got there it was early, about 7 am, and I was afraid someone might try to rob me. So I got my rifle out of my car trunk and stood it up in the back of the bread truck for insurance. Just after I stood it I guess it must have fallen over and discharged accidently. The barrel must have exploded and caused me all this problem,"

Eagle Eye said as he pointed to his still swollen face and left arm. "I was totally knocked out . . . I don't remember anything from then till I woke up in the hospital. I didn't attempt to kill anyone. I've been falsely accused Judge."

Judge Oakes looked over the rim of his glasses toward Sheriff J. Bert Sterling and said, "Sheriff, can you prove what Mr. Looney just said didn't happen?"

"No, your honor, but it sure sounds unlikely to me," Bert replied.

"And to me as well," Judge Oakes said. "But without some evidence to convict him, I have no recourse but to release him."

The judge then looked around his courtroom and said, "Anyone out there have anything to add? Did any of you see Mr. Looney aim his rifle at Sheriff Sterling?"

Quietness filled the courtroom.

"Very well. Mr. Looney, you are hereby again released due to lack of evidence. I would suggest that you try and keep your nose clean."

Eagle Eye replied, "Yes sir, Judge Oakes, I sure will."

Deputy Kyle Potter then walked to Eagle Eye and removed his handcuffs. "I'll do a better job next time of trailing you Eagle Eye. You make one wrong move and I'll be all over you."

Eagle Eye looked at Kyle and said, "Deputy, are you threatening me?"

"No, just giving you some good, sound advice," Kyle replied as Eagle Eye started for the door.

On his way home Eagle Eye thought about his situation. It had now been over a month since Pretty Boy's visit, and he had made two unsuccessful attempts to take out the sheriff. He'd likely be hearing from Pretty Boy very soon, and he might not survive. He got home and, after getting a beer from the fridge, sat in one of the old beat-up chairs in the living room. Just as he was pondering his situation the phone rang.

Eagle Eye picked up the receiver and said, "Hello. If you're selling something, forget it."

A voice on the other end of the line said, "I'm not selling anything, I'm getting ready to collect."

Eagle Eye recognized the voice of Pretty Boy Maggard, and said, "Pretty Boy, I'm so glad to hear from you. I just got home from the hospital. You likely heard that I had a little accident when I tried to shoot the sheriff."

"I heard," responded Pretty Boy, and Eagle Eye could hear him spit a streak of tobacco juice. "I also heard that the sheriff's pussy cat got the best of you."

"That beast he keeps in his office was a big surprise, I just didn't know she was there. And I sure didn't count on that rifle exploding in my face. But I'm going to get him, Pretty Boy, I just need a little more time. I can assure you the third time will be the charm. I've already made plans in my mind how it's going to happen. I'm going to need a little help from Badass Brown, but I won't charge you any extra for that. Just give me a little more time."

"You already had over a month," replied Pretty Boy. "How much more time you need?"

"What I'm planning will take place during a ceremony the city is planning for sometime during the first part of October. Sheriff J. Bert Sterling will be a thing of the past when that ceremony is over," said Eagle Eye. "That suit you?"

Pretty Boy replied, "I probably should have my head examined for ever hiring you in the first place, but I guess I can hold out for another month or so. But understand one thing Eagle Eye. If your third attempt is unsuccessful I won't be calling again on the phone. And you won't ever be talking to anyone again, you understand what I'm saying?"

"I do," said Eagle Eye.

Eagle Eye heard Pretty Boy's phone slam down and then

the dial tone on the other end of the line. A bead of sweat from his brow fell down over the grin on his face. He had just bought a little more time, but he had to make sure his next effort went as planned.

Chapter 27

Harlan, Kentucky

It was Saturday morning. Mayor Fred Knapp sat in his small office at the back of Creech Cafe. He picked up his phone and called Dr. Randy Peters.

"Hello my friend, or are you too famous now to talk to your ole buddy in Harlan?" said Fred into his phone.

Randy replied, "Hello indeed! I take it from that comment that you must have seen on television or read in the newspapers my press conference yesterday?"

Fred said, "Randy, I think everyone in the whole wide world is now very much aware of your most recent acquisition. It was plastered on all the television stations, and front page pictures of you standing behind that lovely Helena Anchor Cross are laying here on my desk in the **Harlan Daily Enterprise** and **The Louisville Courier-Journal**. And I'm sure since the network television news channels picked up the story other newspapers everywhere have carried it as well. Congratulations!"

"Thank you my friend," replied Randy. "I am truly most excited about being able to have the Helena Anchor Cross here in my Center. It will eventually return to either the gentleman that let me borrow it, Mr. Felix Faure, or it will go to its original owner if we establish to Mr. Faure's satisfaction who that is, and get his approval. In the meantime, I'm just delighted to have it here to display and research. And I'll bet with all the new notoriety its gotten you might be interested in having it displayed in Harlan."

"You got that right," Fred replied. "If that's still a possibility I think it would draw enough people to fill the downtown area. It would be a huge boost to our economy, and provide a lot of good press coverage for our town. The Governor has already called me this morning to see if we can get it. Do I understand that you would be willing?"

Randy said, "Of course! You know my love for Harlan, and the other two anchor crosses have a Harlan connection, so I certainly don't see any reason why our new one should not. I'll have to get permission from Mr. Faure, but I think he'll go along with it. As a matter of fact, he plans to come visit me and perhaps we could arrange for him to be here at the time of the Harlan showing. You still planning on the first week-end in October for it?"

"Correct. It looks like Saturday, October 5th will be the date. You think that would work with you and Mr. Faure?" asked Fred.

"I'll be talking with Mr. Faure this weekend and I'll phone you to confirm it just as soon as I get the word from him. That be okay?"

"Couldn't ask for more," replied Fred. "You just don't know how much we all here in Harlan appreciate you, Randy. Thank you so very much. One last thing before we hang up, is everything still on schedule with Raymond? Will you be bringing him back here next week?"

"It is and I will," Randy replied. "He's scheduled to arrive at Blue Grass Field around 1 am on Monday. He's coming in on the same flight I had. I'll pick him up and get him to my home for a long rest. He'll need it after his thirty-six-hour trip. Then I plan to drive him to Harlan next Tuesday. Hope to see you then."

"Sounds great," said Fred. "Betty is scheduled back home this weekend, and I know she will be looking forward greatly to seeing Raymond, and you as well. You take care, and everyone will look forward to seeing you and Raymond next Tuesday, and I'll anticipate a call from you sometime this weekend to, hopefully, okay the Helena Anchor Cross showing in Harlan on October 5th. Good-bye my friend."

"Pax Tecum and good-bye," Randy replied as he hung up his phone.

Just as the Mayor was placing his phone back in its cradle he looked out the window in his office to see Bert and Kyle sitting at a table drinking coffee. He immediately stood and walked out of his office toward them.

"You guys slipped in on me," said Fred as he pulled up a chair and joined Bert and Kyle. "I was in the office talking by phone with Randy Peters."

"You mean the celebrity," said Kyle.

"One and the same," replied Fred. "And it looks real promising that he will be able to bring the new anchor cross to Harlan on October 5th. That should really draw a crowd."

"It should," said Bert. "Have you given thought as to how to display it in the Seibert Anchor Cross memorial? It's a small structure, and the waiting line to view it could be extremely long. Do you plan to limit the time each person has to view?"

Fred replied, "Hey, sheriff, you're already on top of it! Yes, we will keep the line moving right along. Our plans now are to not allow people to actually stop when they reach the Helena Anchor Cross. We'll have officers there to make sure they keep moving. We'll open it at 8 am and be open until 8 pm. I'm sure there will be a long line at times, but people will just have to be a little patient."

"Well, with enough planning I'm sure it will work fine," said Bert as Kyle nodded in agreement.

Fred then told Bert and Kyle about Randy's plans to bring Raymond back to Harlan on Tuesday, and about the possibility that Mr. Faure would be in Harlan along with the Helena Anchor Cross on October 5th.

Bert and Kyle emptied their coffee cups, and Bert said, "Well, Fred, I guess we'd best get back to catching crooks."

Fred replied, "Before you leave, you got time for my latest story?"

"Make it fast ... and funny," Kyle replied.

Fred pointed to a newspaper article he had just this morning posted on his store wall and said, "That article over there was in yesterday's **Knoxville News-Sentinel**. It tells about this couple that lived in Minnesota. They were right in the middle of a brutally cold and nasty winter and decided to take a week's vacation in Florida to get away from the awful weather. Their schedules didn't permit the two of them to travel together, so the guy told his wife he would fly down on Friday, and she could fly down to join him on Saturday. So the husband flew down and got checked into the hotel. There was a computer in the hotel, so the husband decided to send his wife an email. Unfortunately, he left out a letter in his wife's email address and his email went by mistake to a grieving widow in Houston who had just returned from her husband's funeral. He was a minister and had suffered a fatal heart attack. His widow decided to check her email, and when she did she started screaming and then fainted. Her son, who was with her, rushed over to help his mom and looked at the computer screen, which read:

> *To: My loving wife*
>
> *From: Your husband*
>
> *Subject: I've arrived!*
>
> *I know you're surprised to hear from me. They have computers down here now and you are allowed to send emails to your loved ones. I've just arrived and have been*

checked-in. I've seen that everything has been prepared for your arrival tomorrow. Looking forward to seeing you then. I hope your journey is as uneventful as mine was. It sure is hot down here!"

Bert and Kyle got big smiles on their faces. Bert said, "Fred, another good one. I'll try and remember to tell Raymond that one next Tuesday."

As they walked toward the door Polly said, "Bye bye good guys, bye bye good guys."

They each stroked the bird's feathers as they left.

Chapter 28

Victoria, Seychelles

It was Saturday afternoon. Raymond had spent Saturday morning in a meeting with the group of eleven other ministers, the six coordinators, and Bishop David Morgan. The purpose of the meeting was to evaluate the previous two weeks of work, and to allow a chance for everyone to say their good-byes. Each coordinator gave a review of the work of their two ministers, and then reported the number of persons making public professions for Christ. When Peter Alexander made his report, representing Pastor Raymond Bell and Father Elmer Schmidt, he announced that a total of eighty-five souls had accepted Christ publicly, and likely many more had done so privately and would be making their decisions known in the future. After all six coordinators had reported, a grand total of 375 public decisions for Christ were announced by Bishop Morgan. He pronounced the mission trip a great success, and after thanking each of the ministers for their outstanding work he offered a closing prayer. Everyone present then proceeded to seek out friends they had made during their visit and say their good-byes.

Raymond and Elmer Schmidt were leaving on the same flight that evening. They spent the afternoon walking around downtown Victoria and doing a little shopping. They then went to a restaurant that the Bishop had recommended for dinner. During the meal Pastor Bell recalled and related to Father Schmidt the story about the Costello fart. Father Schmidt thought it hilarious! They talked about all the five different sites they had visited, and agreed that the Faure Plantation was perhaps the most interesting with the discovery of the beautiful Anchor Cross. They also agreed that their two last sites, Silhouette and North Islands, were certainly memorable. Silhouette Island had a population of only around 200, but they had filled the small chapel each evening with their services and had twenty-two there to accept Christ. On smaller North Island there were only about fifty residents. It had been developed as a private resort in 2003 with eleven villas for guests. The Duke and Duchess of Cambridge spent their honeymoon on North Island in May, 2011. As with Silhouette Island, the chapel on North Island was small, but filled to capacity each evening. Eleven professions of faith were made on North Island. The two agreed that the two weeks were very, very special, and that they would keep in contact with each other. With dinner concluded the two hailed a cab to the airport, and began their long thirty-six-hour trip back home.

•••

At exactly 1 am Monday morning, Raymond's flight landed at Blue Grass field in Lexington. As he came down the escalator to the luggage claim area Raymond spotted Randy with a big smile on his face and waving wildly. The two embraced, and then chatted nonstop until Raymond's luggage arrived. It was about 2:15 am when they arrived at Randy's home, and they were still so excited that they sat and talked for another half hour after getting into their pajamas. Finally, at about 3 am, the two retired to their bedrooms.

Randy had told Raymond about the plans to take the Helena Anchor Cross to Harlan for the October 5th viewing, and Raymond was greatly pleased to learn the news. He also told Raymond that he had been able to talk with Felix Faure on Sunday and that he had agreed to a two-week visit starting the last week in September, and would accompany him to Harlan for the viewing.

Randy and Raymond had agreed to sleep until about noon. Randy would then prepare a hearty breakfast for them, after which they would travel to Harlan on Tuesday afternoon

Chapter 29

Harlan County, Kentucky

Eagle Eye Looney and Badass Brown sat together drinking beer in Eagle Eye's living room. Eagle Eye's brothers were at work.

"Badass, we've got to figure a way to take out the Sheriff or else I'm in deep dodo. I've tried using a pistol and a rifle, and those didn't work. There's got to be a way . . . you got any ideas?"

After about a minute of pondering and two more sips of beer Badass replied, "Well, I don't think going after him in his office will work. The only other place where we know he will be is at that upcoming cross-thing showing at the court house memorial on October 5th. Maybe we could work up something for him there?"

"That's a possibility. He'll for sure be there, but there'll be a lot more police there as well. You have something specific in mind?" asked Eagle Eye.

Badass said, "Whatever we do will have to be done without guns or knives or anything like that. I'm sure they will have a metal detector that everyone going into the memorial building will have to pass through."

Eagle Eye said, "Yeah, you're right there. So what does that leave for us?"

"You know I spent most of my life in the bug exterminating business," replied Badass. "So I know a little something about how to handle chemicals. I'm sure I could come up with a system that could be worn that could spray something on the sheriff, something maybe like sulfuric acid. That stuff is really nasty."

Eagle Eye took another large swallow of beer and said, "I think you're onto something. I've been embarrassed by the sheriff a couple of times now, so some way to do him in that would cause a lot of pain would be right in order. How could we do this?"

Badass finished his beer and reached into the cooler sitting between them and extracted another can. After opening it and taking a long swallow said, "We gotta be careful. That stuff is deadly. First, we need to get some. Trigger Green will sell it to us, he keeps a good supply to remove serial numbers off guns and car parts. Then I would put together a spray system that didn't have any metal in it and could be worn without being obvious. The nozzle would come out the end of the shirt sleeve, and when it was ready to be used the person wearing it would just open a valve with one hand and then point the nozzle toward the sheriff."

"Sounds complicated," Eagle Eye responded. "And let's get one thing straight right now. It would have to be you wearing this thing. The moment the sheriff saw me he'd know something was up. I'll bet he hasn't seen you in years."

"I do try and avoid him," Badass replied. "You know me, anything for a friend for a fee! How much would this be worth to you?"

Eagle Eye thought to himself, 'It'd be worth my life!', and then said, "Badass, I could scrape up $2500. I'd like to offer more, but that's all I got. What d'you say?"

After another swig Badass said, "Since we're good pals, I'll do it. But only if we work out a plan that will allow me to get away and not be identified. I sure don't want to spend the rest of my life in the pokey for $2500."

Eagle Eye reached his right hand over to Badass and they shook hands for about thirty seconds. Eagle Eye then said, "So now it's a done deal. I'll give you half now, and the other half after we've pulled it off . . . that okay?"

"That'll work," replied Badass. "Here's what we'll do. First thing is to get the acid. Since you've made a couple of trips to Maggard's recently for the guns, I probably should go for the acid. I'll tell them I've got a bunch of car parts that I want to remove the serial numbers from. I'll try and buy a quart, I'm sure we won't need that much but we might spill some in getting everything set up. After we got the acid I'll put together the spray system, and then we'll try it out with water to make sure it works. You can be working on the plan for how we pull this off without getting caught. We've got almost a month, so that should be plenty of time. How's that sound?"

"Perfect," replied Eagle Eye. "You sit tight a minute." He then got up and walked into his bedroom and removed $1250 from the box in his footlocker, carried it back into the living room, handed it to Badass and said, "Whatever the acid costs I'll pay you back for it."

Badass got a big grin on his face, counted the money, took another sip of beer, and said "I'm off to Maggards … might as well get started." He emptied his beer can, and walked out the front door.

•••

Fatso Chapel saw him coming. There weren't too many old, faded-out Bunny Bread trucks still operating in Harlan County … as a matter of fact Fatso knew of none other than the one driven by Badass Brown.

The front door opened and Badass walked into Maggard's Grocery.

"Well, well, well, if it isn't ole Badass Brown," Fatso exclaimed.

"Morning Fatso, long time no see," replied Badass. "I need to make a little purchase. Trigger in?"

Fatso replied, "Yeah, he's in. What should I tell him you're in the market for?"

"Little acid," Badass replied.

"Dope or Sulfuric?" Fatso responded.

"Sulfuric, you know I don't do no drugs Fatso," said Badass.

"I'll tell him," Fatso replied as he hit the intercom to Trigger and said, "Hey Trigger, a Mr. Badass Brown is here to see you about purchasing a little sulfuric acid."

"Tell him to come on back," Trigger replied over the intercom.

Fatso pressed the button below the counter to open the door to Trigger's office, and then said, "Hey Badass, you know why elephants wear pink tennis shoes?"

Badass replied with a smile, "You got me there, Fatso."

"They wear pink tennis shoes because white ones get dirty too fast," said Fatso with a giggle.

Badass walked into Trigger's office and said, "Good morning Trigger, how's tricks?"

Trigger remained seated at his desk and looked up at Badass, "Okay. What can I do for you?"

"Right to business, huh," Badass replied. "Well, I need to get a quart of sulfuric acid. I've got a bunch of car parts with serial numbers that need to disappear. Think you can help me with that?"

"I think we have that in our inventory," Trigger replied with a grin. "It'll cost you $150."

"Deal," said Badass as he peeled out the money and handed it to Trigger.

Trigger then stood and walked over to a closet and removed a quart glass jar full of the acid and then walked back to Badass and handed it to him, "Better be real careful that jar don't get busted.....you want a box with some packing in it?"

"If that's part of the $150 I'd appreciate it," Badass replied with a smile.

Trigger hit the intercom and said, "Hey Fatso, our customer is coming out with a jar of product, could you please pack it for him in a box?"

"Will do, boss," replied Fatso.

"Be careful Badass. See you around," said Trigger.

"Yeah," Badass replied as he turned and left Trigger's office.

Chapter 30

Lexington, Kentucky

Randy and Raymond slept like logs. Although they intended to arise by noon, they slept soundly until almost 1 pm on Tuesday. Randy then prepared a super "breakfast" for them, and after enjoying the meal and getting dressed and all packed they headed out for Harlan. The three hour trip provided them additional time to do the chit-chat and get all caught up on the activities of the past few days.

•••

Betty came running out the front door of her home and

gave Raymond a big hug and kiss, then gave Randy a hug and said, "It's just wonderful to have you two world travelers back. Everyone in Harlan is talking about Raymond's mission trip to the Seychelles, and then all that press coverage about the new anchor cross. Come on in and get comfortable. I'll get you some lemonade, and then we can talk. But do let me warn you, I've invited our friends over this evening at 7 pm to hear all about your trips and the Helena Anchor Cross, so unless you want to repeat yourselves, you might wish to save your stories until then."

"Betty, I'm really pleased you did that. I was wondering how we could go about updating our Harlan friends about our trips, and now I find you've already solved that problem. Thank you very much, I'll look forward greatly to sharing our stories this evening," Randy said.

Raymond added, "Honey, did you have a good trip to Florida? Hope you got to see and visit with all your friends and relatives there."

"I did indeed," Betty replied. "And that's something we can talk about before everyone else arrives . . . I wouldn't want to bore them with my little insignificant trip and stories." Betty had a grin on her face as she said that.

"Nothing could be further from the truth," said Randy. "Everyone's equally interested to hear about your trip. We'll have a grand time of sharing this evening."

•••

At approximately 7:15 pm Kyle walked into the Bell's living room along with his mother Carolyn. They were the last of the expected guests to arrive. Betty had provided several trays of "finger food" for everyone. In addition to Raymond and Betty, Kyle, Carolyn, Fred, and Randy were all standing in the living room talking when Raymond said, "Friends, it is indeed a joyous occasion to have such a gathering this evening. I wonder if you would join me in a prayer before we start updating everyone about the events of the past couple of weeks."

All joined hands and Raymond blessed the gathering. They then took their seats, and Raymond said, "Let me first say that I know things have been happening here in Harlan since Randy and I have been gone, and we certainly want to hear all about those. But since someone has to go first I thought I'd tell you a bit about my mission trip, then let Randy update you on his very brief trip the Seychelles and the beautiful new anchor cross, and then, Fred, maybe you could take the lead in telling us what has been going on here in Harlan. Does that sound okay to everyone?"

All nodded in agreement. Raymond took about forty-five minutes to review his mission trip, including discussions about each of the five different sites he and Father Schmidt visited. He then discussed the "wrap-up" meeting last Saturday morning in Victoria with Bishop Morgan, the other eleven ministers, and the six coordinators. When he announced that 85 decisions had been made for Christ as a result of his and Father Schmidt's services, and that a total of 375 decisions had been made from all six teams, applause broke out and many "Amen's" were heard. Next Randy updated everyone on the discovery of the anchor cross, his trip to visit the plantation of Felix Faure, and the decision by Mr. Faure to allow him to bring the anchor cross back to his Center for display and study. He also told everyone of Mr. Faure's plans to come to Kentucky sometime during the last week of this month, and that he would be staying until after the Harlan viewing of the Helena Anchor Cross. Mayor Fred Knapp then reviewed the plans for the October 5th showing. He stated that the Governor and Economic Development Secretary were both very pleased about the upcoming event, and that they planned to be in attendance. Fred said that work had already begun on the Seibert Anchor Cross memorial building to enhance it to accommodate the large crowd of people anticipated to attend. Bert then talked about the security that would be in place for the event, and that he was coordinating everything with both the Harlan City Police and the Kentucky State Police. They had plans in place to both handle the anticipated large number of vehicles, and to monitor the crowd to make sure everything came off smoothly. He further stated that everyone in line to go into the memorial would pass through a metal detector to assure that no weapons were brought inside the building.

There were then a lot of questions back and forth within the group, and all of Betty's "finger food" disappeared. At about 11 pm Raymond said, "Friends, I think we've had a super visit together this evening. I appreciate so much each of you being here. The hour is getting a little late for some of us older persons, so perhaps the time has come to say good-bye for now, and we'll look forward to another gathering before long. Randy plans an early start back to Lexington in the morning, and we all have to get back to our jobs early tomorrow, so thanks again for being here, and have a safe trip home."

Chapter 31

Harlan, Kentucky

It was 7 am. Deputy Kyle Potter walked into the sheriff's department to check his mail before driving to Eagle Eye's house to tail him for the day.

"Hey Bert," Kyle shouted through the open door into the sheriff's office. "I just stopped by to check my mail."

Bert walked into the front office and said, "Well, the early bird gets the worm. You're certainly early this morning. Anything been going on with Eagle Eye lately?"

"Nothing," replied Kyle. "He just hangs out at his house. His brothers go to work every day and Badass Brown usually drops by with a six-pack of beer. I guess they just sit in the house watching television, drinking beer, and swapping stories. I don't think Eagle Eye has even left his house for the past several days. Sure makes my job boring. I'm really getting caught up on my reading. I've gone through about seven paperbacks in the past week. I'm beginning to think it a waste of the taxpayer's money for me to be sitting there."

"I understand," Bert replied. "Why don't you just finish up this week staked-out on him, and then next week come on back to your normal job. You can then stick around close with me for another week or two. After that I would think everything would be okay."

Kyle replied, "Sounds like a plan to me. I'm off to keep an eye on Eagle Eye!"

• • •

Kyle parked in his usual secluded spot. He had a good vantage point to see Eagle Eye's house, but was far enough away that he wouldn't be spotted. His spot was also enough off the road that cars coming and going didn't see him parked in his private car. He started reading his latest paperback. At about 9 am Badass Brown's bread van arrived at the house and

Badass emerged with an old suitcase in one hand and a six-pack of beer in the other. He entered the house.

"Mornin Eagle Eye," Badass said as he sat the suitcase and beer down. "I've got our system all worked out. Why don't we sit here and have a beer or two and then I'll put it on and we can try it out . . . using water rather than acid, of course."

"Okay by me," Eagle Eye replied as he reached for a beer. The two sat drinking beer for the next hour. Finally Eagle Eye said, "Well, I think the time has come to see what kind of a gizmo you've come up with."

"Time for the unveiling," replied Badasss and he reached down and opened the suitcase. He reached into it, grabbed the contraption, held it up and said, "This is it!! This baby will do in the sheriff of Harlan County!"

Eagle Eye looked at Badass with a frown on his face and said, "Don't look very lethal to me."

"Please allow me to demonstrate," Badass replied. He then strapped the contraption on himself. It consisted of a pair of suspenders with a large, flat glass flask ducktaped across the suspenders in the back. One end of the flask was fitted with tubing that ran to a small plastic air cylinder that Badass was strapping on the back of his left leg with more ducktape. The other end of the flask was fitted with a valve and then about three feet of tubing which terminated in a nozzle. Badass used more ducktape to strap the tubing along the bottom of his left shoulder and arm. The nozzle then hung at the bottom of his left wrist. When finished he reached into the suitcase and pulled out an old wrinkled and thread-bare sport coat and put it on.

"How do I look?" He asked Eagle Eye.

"Like a street bum," replied Eagle Eye.

"But you can't tell I'm wearing this thing, can you?" said Badass

"I see that cylinder thing strapped to your left leg," said Eagle Eye.

"Of course you do . . . but when we do it I'll have it strapped to my bare leg under my pants. Today is just for demonstration, understand?" replied Badass.

"Okay, okay," said Eagle Eye. "So how does it work?"

"Watch closely," Badass replied. "First, the glass flask is filled with water today, but when we do the job it'll be filled with acid. So I grab the nozzle with my left hand, like this, and then with my right hand I reach around toward my right rear pants pocket, like I was reaching for my handkerchief. I then just reach up and turn the valve with my right hand while I point the nozzle with my left hand. Water started spurting out the nozzle in a full stream. Badass had the nozzle pointed toward Eagle Eye and the stream of water hit him directly in the face."

"Damn it, Badass, you done squirted me. I can't see nothing," yelled Eagle Eye.

"Yeah. Just be glad that was water and not acid. Else you'd really have something to yell about," replied Badass.

"Hey, that worked pretty good," Eagle Eye replied. "How exactly did it work?"

"Well, dummy, I just explained it to you. When I turned the valve I let the water flow into the tubing. It was forced by the air pressure hooked up to the other end. All we got to do to be ready for the real thing is to hook up a new air cylinder and then fill the flask with sulfuric acid. Then when I turn that valve the acid will shoot out the nozzle. Understand?" said Badass.

"You smart man," said Eagle Eye, wiping the water from his eyes and face. "But I got a question. When that acid hits the tubing and nozzle won't it eat through them?"

"It will, but not that fast. We'll be able to squirt all the acid through the nozzle before it has a chance to eat a hole in them.

I won't get any acid on me. It should work like a charm," replied Badass.

"It sure did work great with water," Eagle Eye replied. "Once it hits ole Bert in the face how long does he have?"

"It'll eat right through flesh like it wasn't even there ... likely go right into his brain," said Badass. "He'll start screaming and all that, but he'll be a goner real quick."

"Got to hand it to you, Badass, I think you've come up with exactly what we need."

"That's my end of the deal. Your end was to come up with some way to assure that I'm able to get away. You given that any thought?" said Badass.

"Sure have. Here's how it's going to work. I'm going to get ole Bennie, the town drunk, to do a little 'mooning' for us," replied Eagle Eye.

"I don't understand. You'll have to explain," said Badass.

"Well, I'll give Bennie a fifth of whiskey and tell him he'll get two more just for pulling a little prank for me. I'll tell him to get in line to see the cross-thing. You will be in line two people in front of him. I'll tell him just as soon as you get through the metal detector and inside the building to just drop his pants, bend over, and moon everyone behind in line.

That'll be the distraction we need. All the cops and everyone else will be all focused on ole Bennie. When that happens you just do your thing with the acid and then run out the other end of the memorial. Once you get outside there'll be enough people all around that you won't even be noticed. You can then just walk calmly to wherever you parked your van and drive away. Should work slick as a ribbon!"

Badass thought about that for a minute, and then said, "Should work. Let's have another beer and think about it."

Chapter 32

Prestonsburg, Kentucky

It was a grimy little gas station just off Highway 23, about one mile south of Prestonsburg in East Central Kentucky. Big Jim Owens was the owner, and had an office in the back. Big Jim was Floyd County's largest drug dealer, and into anything else that might make him money. About thirteen years ago he had lost $200,000 when one of his drivers lost control of his car and struck a tree and was killed on his way to deliver the money to Pretty Boy Maggard. Pretty Boy would have laundered the money for Big Jim, but it was lost when the police found it at the wreck site. Then later that year Big Jim lost about a half million more when a bank robbery was aborted and two lock boxes belonging to Pretty Boy were found to have 3.5 million dollars in illegal drug money. He still had not gotten over those losses.

Big Jim sat behind his filthy desk, feet propped up and smoking a cigar. Sitting on the other side of the desk was one of his cronies, Mad Mike Hatfield. Big Jim said, "Mad Mike, you been seeing all that stuff on television and in the newspapers about that new anchor cross thing that the fellow at the University of Kentucky got?"

"Couldn't miss it, Big Jim," Mad Mike replied. "It's been the main news now for several days. That thing must be worth a fortune."

"Exactly my thought," Big Jim said. "A mighty big fortune at that, I'll bet."

"Got any ideas on how we might be able to get our hands on it?" asked Mad Mike.

Big Jim replied, "As a matter of fact, I do. It just so happens that I've got a snitch that works for the University as a janitor in that Center that houses the anchor cross. It's called the Center for Appalachian Research, or CAR. I called him yesterday to see if he might come up with a little information for us."

"What kind of information," asked Mad Mike.

"Well, if you've been watching the news you know that the Governor has planned a viewing of that anchor cross in Harlan on October 5th. I'll just be willing to bet that the Director of the CAR, a fellow named Dr. Randy Peters, will be transporting the anchor cross to Harlan. If so, that means that sometime probably on Friday, the day before the showing, he will likely be driving to Harlan and have that very valuable anchor cross with him. Now just suppose that we could find out from our snitch what time Dr. Peters would be leaving Lexington and what his car looks like.....maybe even the license number. Now if we knew all that information I bet we could set something up to relieve him of that valuable anchor cross. What'd you think Mad Mike?" asked Big Jim.

Mad Mike thought for a minute and said, "I'm sure we could. What would we do with it once we had it? From what I hear on the news, it's pretty much a one of a kind thing. Might be a little hard to fence."

"I thought about that too," replied Big Jim. "We would hold it for ransom. I'm sure the state would pay major bucks to have it back in time for the showing in Harlan the following day. All we would have to do would be to call the sheriff's office and tell them we wanted two million dollars in cash by midnight on

Friday, and work out some way to exchange the anchor cross for the cash. I think it would work."

"Sounds good to me," Mad Mike said. "We need to work on all the details, but seems to me that around midnight on October 4th we could be two million dollars richer!"

Big Jim leaned back a little further in his chair, took a big puff on his cigar, and got a real big grin on his face.

Chapter 33

Harlan, Kentucky

Mayor Knapp, Sheriff Sterling, and Deputy Potter all sat together at a back table in Creech Cafe.

Mayor Knapp said, "Gentleman, things are really coming together well for our upcoming October 5th viewing of the Helena Anchor Cross. The publicity that Randy generated for it has truly been a blessing. I understand that all the motels in Harlan and Bell counties are booked solid for that weekend. It looks as though we could have a record number of people here in Harlan. We're just a couple of weeks away now, and I'm starting to get a little nervous that something might have been overlooked. My understanding is that Randy will be bringing Mr. Felix Faure and the anchor cross to Harlan on Friday, October 4th. The Bells have graciously invited the two of them to stay as house guests for the weekend. That should work real well. You guys have everything along the security line all set up?"

Bert replied, "I think so. We've coordinated with the Harlan and State Police. The Governor and Economic Secretary plan to arrive around 11 am on the 5th. They'll be escorted in by the State Police and we'll park them behind the court house. We're not having any public speeches that day, so that simplifies things a lot. Governor Shear and Secretary O'Malley will just walk immediately from their car to the memorial Building for the viewing. I'm sure folks won't mind them bucking the line. I know they'll be doing all kinds of waving and handshaking before they go inside and view the anchor cross. I don't think that should present any security problem, they'll be well escorted with State Police. We have a schedule for all the law enforcement personnel, and I think we have the traffic and the security ends all covered."

"Fred, will you be joining the Governor and Secretary when they get here?" asked Kyle.

Fred replied, "Yes, I do plan to try and greet them when

they arrive and will walk with them through the memorial. I figured I should do that, since I'm mayor."

"Yes, that would certainly be appropriate," Bert replied. "When will Randy and Mr. Faure arrive at the memorial?"

Fred said, "The memorial is scheduled to open for viewing at 8 am. So they will be asked to be there no later than 7:30 to get things all arranged. I've asked Kyle if he would be so kind as to escort them from the Bell's home to the memorial. That Helena Anchor Cross is priceless, and I sure wouldn't want anything to happen to it. Kyle will assure that it stays safe. Also I understand that you, Bert, will be at the memorial starting at about 7:30 as well. Is that correct?"

Bert replied, "You got it. I'll definitely be there when Kyle arrives with the anchor cross, Randy, and Raymond. My plans are to be there most of the day. I'll slip out sometime for a little lunch, but otherwise I want to be real close in case there's any trouble. Kyle and I will both be there inside the memorial behind the display that houses the anchor cross. We'll likely be standing most of the time, but will have chairs to sit occasionally if we get tired."

"Great," Fred responded. "Speaking of the display, I feel real good about it. We spent quite a few bucks getting one made that will safely and securely house the anchor cross, but still enable those viewing to see it in all its beauty. The display case is made of thick plexiglas and the anchor cross will sit on a pedestal that revolves. It will make one full revolution about every fifteen seconds, so folks walking through to view it should get to see it from all sides. We also have nice spot lighting set up to shine on it. As you know, we'll have officers there to keep the line moving. People won't be allowed to stop . . . that would just take too much time. They'll enter the building through the door on the South side and exit through the North side door. The metal detector will be set up just inside the South side door."

"What if we have rain on the 5th?" asked Kyle.

"No problem inside the building, of course, and those outside will just have to use umbrellas or raingear. Let's keep our fingers crossed for a beautiful, sunny fall day," replied Fred.

Fred then added, "You know, I feel really good about this. I think Harlan will greatly benefit, and that our fair city will make news everywhere on October 5th. So now before you guys have to get back to work can I tell you my latest story?"

Kyle looked at Bert and said, "I thought maybe you might have one for us . . . go right ahead Mr. Mayor."

Fred started by pointing at an article posted on the wall behind Bert. He said, "You see that article there with the picture of the wrecked car? That article was in the **Harlan Daily Enterprise** just last week. Apparently a lady ran a red light at the corner of Central and Main Streets. She crashed into a car driven by a man. Both cars were demolished, but amazingly neither the man or woman was hurt. After they crawled out of their cars, the woman says, 'Wow, just look at our cars! There's nothing left, but fortunately we are not hurt. This must be a sign from God that we should meet and be friends and live together in peace for the rest of our days.' The man replies, ' I agree with you completely. This must be a sign from God!' The woman continues, 'And look at this, here's another miracle. My car is completely demolished, but my bottle of wine didn't break. Surely God wants us to drink this wine and celebrate our good fortune.' She then handed the bottle to the man. The man nods his head in agreement, opens it, drinks half the bottle and then hands it back to the woman. The woman takes the bottle, puts the cap back on, and hands it back to the man. The man asks, 'Aren't you having any?' The woman replies, 'Nah, I think I'll just wait for the police!'

Bert and Kyle both laugh heartily, and then Bert said, "Men will never learn!"

Kyle said, "Thanks Fred, another one to remember."

The two officers then stood, shook hands with Fred, and headed back to the office.

Chapter 34

Lexington, Kentucky

Felix Faure had arrived in Lexington almost a week ago and had enjoyed being Randy's house guest. The two of them had spent their days at the Center for Appalachian Research where Randy had gotten Felix updated on his research related to the Helena Anchor Cross. During their time not at the Center Randy showed Felix all the beautiful horse farms and attractions in and around Lexington.

It was Friday, October 4th, and the two had left Lexington about two hours ago headed for Harlan. Since their trip began Randy had regaled Felix about the history and beauty of Harlan County. Also, he told Felix about all the events associated with the Seibert and Pelle anchor crosses. They were both looking forward greatly to getting to Harlan and staying with Raymond and Betty Bell, and then to displaying the Helena Anchor Cross tomorrow. It should be an exciting weekend.

They had turned off Highway 25E onto Highway 119 at Pineville ten miles ago. They were currently about twenty miles from Harlan.

Randy glanced into his rear view mirror and noticed a large, black Chevrolet Suburban coming up behind them.

"That's them," said Mad Mike. "The make and color of their car matches, and so does the license numbers. Your Lexington snitch sure came through for us. I think it's about show time."

Big Jim and Mad Mike were dressed in police uniforms. They had been waiting in a drive way a couple of miles back. When Randy's car passed they had pulled out behind them.

Big Jim was driving. He always liked to be in control, and didn't trust anyone else at the wheel. He said, "Yeah, no doubt about it . . . that's them. Just as soon as we get around this next curve there's a long straight stretch. When we get there I'll pull up real close behind them and you put the blue light on the dash and turn it and the siren on. We'll pull 'em over."

Randy said, "Felix, there's a car coming up behind us that

looks like police. I don't know anything I've done wrong . . . I haven't been speeding. Hope it's not trouble."

Felix turned to look behind them just as the siren sounded and the blue light started flashing on the car's dash. He said, "Yep, it's the police. Looks like they want us to pull over."

Randy dropped his speed and then slowly pulled his car well off the road onto the wide shoulder and stopped. The car behind him did the same.

"Why are you holding your cell phone up to your ear?" Mad Mike asked Big Jim.

"They're watching us, and this looks like I'm checking out their license plate before we get out. That's always what the cops do," replied Big Jim.

"That's using the ol' noodle," replied Mad Mike.

After about a minute Big Jim and Mad Mike opened their car doors and got out. Each put on his fake police hat and they started walking toward Randy's car, Big Jim on the driver's side and Mad Mike on the passenger side.

Randy and Felix had each rolled down their windows.

Big Jim walked up, bent down, and said to Randy, "Good morning gentlemen. I hope I didn't alarm you. Could you please show me your driver's license and proof of insurance."

Randy replied as he reached for his billfold and then opened the glove compartment to get the insurance card, "Certainly officer, just give me a second. I hope we didn't violate any laws."

"No, no," said Big Jim as he looked at the license and insurance card and noticed that the man was indeed Dr. Randy Peters. "Officer Jones and I are part of an illegal drug task force and we just pulled you over at random to check for drugs. Would you please both step out of the vehicle. It should only take a minute or so. Please just step over into the grass beside your car."

Randy and Felix complied. Big Jim and Mad Mike then searched the inside of the car, and then opened the trunk and looked there. They opened the suitcases, and then closed them. They then walked over beside Randy and Felix, and Big Jim reached down and drew his pistol and held it pointed at the two.

Randy and Felix each immediately raised their hands with looks of shock on their faces. Randy said, "Officers, we've done nothing wrong. There must be some mistake here."

Big Jim responded, "No mistake, Dr. Peters, we're looking for that valuable anchor cross. We know you have it. Hand it over peacefully and no one will get hurt. If you don't, then you two will be pushing up daisies in short order."

Big Jim and Mad Mike were standing about ten feet away from and facing Randy and Felix. Randy replied, "Please, we don't want trouble. I'm wearing the anchor cross on a necklace about my neck. It's under my shirt and sport coat. Would you like me to pull it out?"

"By all means, very carefully," replied Big Jim. "And don't worry about not having it for the big shindig in Harlan tomorrow. You'll get it back just as soon as we get two million dollars in cash. I'll call the sheriff's office with the details of how that will happen."

As Big Jim was talking, Randy had unbuttoned his shirt and pulled out the Helena Anchor Cross and let it fall in view on his chest.

Big Jim then nodded at Mad Mike and said, "Hey, okay, that looks real pretty. Relieve Dr. Peters of his charming necklace."

Mad Mike then walked up to Randy and grabbed the anchor cross tightly with his right hand and started to pull its necklace up and over Randy's head. Smoke and a terrible flesh burning smell then came immediately from Mad Mike's right hand. He jerked his smoking hand free of the anchor cross and turned, doubled up over his injured hand, and started screaming and cursing as he staggered slowly back toward Big Jim.

Big Jim said, "Okay, so much for the easy way." He then pointed his pistol at Randy and fired. No one would remember clearly what happened next, but certainly the bullet was somehow deflected from Randy and ricocheted to hit Mad Mike in the buttocks. He immediately straightened out, grabbed his rear quarter, and fell to the ground moaning.

Big Jim then fired another shot at Randy. This time the bullet miraculously and without explanation bounced from Randy back into Big Jim's right leg. He screamed in pain, and almost lost his balance, but managed to get back into his car while keeping the pistol pointed in the direction of Randy and Felix. Big Jim then shouted to Mad Mike, "Get in the car, get in the car . . . I'm getting out of here. That cross-thing's jinxed us."

Mad Mike, still moaning and cursing, staggered to the car and got in. Luckily, he had left the door open so he didn't have to try and use his quickly swelling right hand. He pulled the door shut with his left hand as Big Jim tromped down on the accelerator and the black Suburban shot onto the road, wheels screeching, dust and rock flying everywhere.

"Did you get their license number?" asked Felix.

"No, but it doesn't matter. I'm sure it was stolen from another car anyway," replied Randy. "Let's get out of here."

The two got back in their car and resumed their trip to Harlan. Randy said, "Felix, I'm so sorry that happened. Not a good way to introduce you to Harlan County."

Felix said, "Hey, it certainly wasn't your fault. And besides, neither of us got hurt. How did that happen?"

"My friend, I think you were just an eyewitness to the amazing, mysterious, and unexplainable power of the Helena Anchor Cross! Because I was wearing it, I was never in doubt about our safety. Pax Tecum indeed! Peace was with us!" replied Randy.

"Well, those police imposters were certainly right about one thing. It only took a minute or so!", said Felix.

Randy said, "Yeah, we should arrive in Harlan about on time, and we'll certainly have a story to tell!"

Randy then reached for his cell phone and speed-dialed his friend Sheriff J. Bert Sterling. Bert answered and Randy related to him their experience with the police imposters, described their vehicle, and reported that each of them had been wounded and that one had serious burns on one hand. Bert thanked

Randy for the report and said that he would immediately alert his officers as well as the Kentucky State Police. They would be looking for a vehicle matching the description with two persons inside wearing police uniforms.

• • •

Big Jim got the Suburban up to speeds close to 100 mph. He knew that Randy Peters would call in a report, and was mad at himself for not grabbing their cell phones. Too much happened too fast. At any rate, he knew he was only about 10 miles from Wallins and Maggard's grocery. He knew if he could get there without being caught he could likely hide the Suburban and get another car from Trigger Green.

"Well, well, well. Look what the cat drug in," Fatso said as Big Jim and Mad Mike staggered in the front door of Maggard's grocery. "Looks like you boys are ailing a bit."

"Shut up Fatso," said Big Jim. "Just push the button to let us in the back room to talk with Trigger."

"I will just as soon as you tell me what a bald elephant wears for a toupee?" said Fatso.

Big Jim and Mad Mike stared at Fatso with looks like they could kill him.

"A bald elephant wears a sheep for a toupee," Fatso said with a grin as he punched the button opening the door to Trigger's office.

Trigger got up from his desk and came around to greet the two as they entered his office. He noticed blood on both their pants, and that Mad Mike was holding his right hand, which appeared to be badly swollen. Trigger asked, "What in the world happened to you two?"

Big Jim related their story to Trigger. It was all Trigger could do from laughing out loud when he heard that Mad Mike had been shot in the rear. Trigger then said, "That sure is a sad story, and I'm all sorry things didn't go as planned for you. But how can I help you?"

Big Jim said, "Main thing is we need a car. Can't drive the suburban, I'm sure they called it in to the cops. I parked it in back of the grocery. The title's in the glove compartment. I've already signed it over to you in exchange for any kind of dinky little car to get us back to Prestonsburg. We can get medical help when we get there . . . we couldn't go to the hospital here in Harlan, they'd call the gun wounds in to the cops."

Trigger replied, "I believe I can help you Big Jim. I just happen to have a thirty-year-old Ford pick-up that I'll trade you. I know it'll get you to Prestonsburg . . . probably not much further. You think you can drive it okay?"

"Don't have much choice. Where is it?" said Big Jim.

Trigger pressed the intercom key to Fatso and said, "Hey Fatso. Customers have bought that old Ford pick up. How about running down and getting it for them?"

Fatso replied, "Will do boss. Just take a minute."

"It's just parked a couple of blocks away.....Fatso will have it for you by the time you walk back to the front of the store. You boys take care," said Trigger.

Big Jim and Mad Mike started to slowly make their way to the parking lot and then back to Prestonsburg.

•••

Randy and Felix arrived at the Bell's home, and after greetings and hugs Betty served a light lunch. The talk during lunch focused on the unfortunate attempted robbery, but Raymond was quick to point out that once again the mysterious power protecting anyone wearing one of the Savior's Crosses had clearly been demonstrated.

Just after the foursome had finished their lunch the doorbell rang and Raymond escorted Bert, Kyle, and Fred into his home. Everyone took a seat in the living room. Discussions followed about Felix's visit with Randy, the attempted robbery, and finally to the upcoming viewing the following day.

Sheriff Sterling reported that the black Suburban had not been found, and likely the would be robbers had managed to get away. Fred went over all the plans for the viewing, and answered a lot of questions. Everything seemed well in order for the big day tomorrow.

Chapter 35

Harlan, Kentucky

It was 7 am on Saturday, October 5th. Dawn was breaking. The sky was clear, and the forecast couldn't have been better . . . clear with a high of seventy-two degrees.

Fred was talking with Sheriff Sterling as they stood beside the doughboy on the front lawn of the Court house. "Bert, we're off to a great start. The weather's going to be chamber of commerce perfect and everything seems all lined up. It looks like all the media are here," as he pointed toward the bank of satellite trucks parked along First Street beside the court house.

Bert replied, "Yeah, I'd say Harlan is going to be in the news tonight. It was a good idea you had to open the memorial to media only starting at 8 am, and then to the public as soon as we can flush out all the media . . . that should be no later than about 8:30. Kyle has already left to pick up Randy, Raymond, and Felix. He'll have them back here no later than 7:30. They'll have at least a half hour to get everything all set up. Got any news from the Governor and Secretary?"

"No. And no news is good news. I assume all is as scheduled with them," replied Fred.

"People are starting to get in line already. There must be at least a dozen there now. I hope they can stand for a while."

"They all look young," Bert replied. "I think they'll make it."

•••

Kyle's patrol car pulled to a stop on Second Street beside the court house. The four guys got out and walked over to where Fred and Bert were standing by the doughboy. Kyle nodded toward the other three guys and said, "Here's my delivery, all safe and sound."

Fred said, "Even a few minutes early. You did well Deputy Potter! Randy, you got the Helena Anchor Cross?"

Randy patted his chest and said, "You bet. I'm wearing it so we would be sure to make it without problems," he said with a smile.

Fred continued, "Mr. Faure, I'll bet even in the Seychelles you don't have weather any nicer than we've got here today."

Felix replied, "You're right. This is grand. And everything looks so nice. Congratulations Mr. Mayor on putting it all together."

"I can't take all the credit," Fred replied. "Unless it's election time, of course, and then I might consider it," he said with a chuckle. "The City of Harlan is just so thankful to you for allowing this viewing of the remarkable anchor cross. Without your consent we wouldn't be having this today. I'm sure the Governor and Secretary will be anxious to extend their thanks also."

"I'll look forward to meeting them," Felix replied.

Bert then said, "I think we should probably get over to the memorial and get everything all set up. The media will be pounding on the door at 8 am sharp to get in and take pictures. We need to be ready."

All six men then proceeded to walk over to the door of the memorial. The technician was checking out the metal detector as they passed through it. The guns carried by Bert and Kyle set it off. They gave a thumbs up sign to the technician. Bert, Kyle, Felix, and Randy then walked behind the long counter that contained the display case in the center of it. Fred and Raymond stayed on the outside of the counter. Fred took a screwdriver and opened the top of the plexiglass enclosure, and then looked at Randy and said, "Well, my friend, it's now time for you to remove your necklace and place the Helena Anchor Cross in our display case."

Randy said, "I can do that," and reached up with both hands and grabbed the necklace and raised it above his head. He then removed the necklace and handed the anchor cross to Fred to place in the display case. Raymond reached over and lightly ran his fingers over both sides of the beautiful artifact. Tears again formed in his eyes as he reflected on the history behind what his fingers were touching. Fred then placed the bottom of the artifact in the slot in the revolving pedestal and then replaced the display top and secured it in place with the screws. The spot lights were then turned on along with the motor for the pedestal. The Helena Anchor Cross then started to rotate, and the spot lights gave it a beautiful, surrealistic appearance. It was all set for viewing.

Fred then looked at his watch. It was 5 minutes before 8 am. He said, "Okay guys, it's just about show time. I think it would be best if Randy and Felix stood directly behind the anchor cross, with Bert on one end and Kyle on the other end. That way we've got the security on each end and Randy and Felix right behind the display to answer questions."

Kyle stepped to the front end of the line behind the counter, and Bert walked to the other end. Randy was standing next to Kyle and Felix next to Bert. So when the media and the public started to pass through the memorial they would first pass through the metal detector at the entrance door on the South side, proceed through the memorial, and then exit through the door on the North side. They would see behind the counter first Officer Potter, then Dr. Peters, then Felix Faure, and finally Sheriff Sterling. The display case rested in the center of the counter, directly between Randy and Felix.

Fred then shouted, "Okay guys, it's 8 am, so let's open the doors to the media."

The technician at the metal detector then opened the South entrance door and media personnel started to enter the memorial. Television and print media were present. The television reporters were all accompanied by their cameramen with cameras mounted on their shoulders. All the print media carried their own cameras on straps about their necks. The oohs and ahhs then started, followed by the clicking of the camera shutters, the rolling of the television cameras, and the almost continuous flashing from the cameras. Questions abounded to both Randy and Felix. They were asked about various features of the Helena Anchor Cross. They pointed to the features as they answered the questions and had their pictures taken. This continued for a little more than 30 minutes. Fred then declared that the media time was over and asked them to please depart from the memorial so that the public could be allowed their turn. Raymond and Fred helped usher them out. When all were gone, Fred said, "Okay, we're now ready for the public viewing …. please open the doors." The public streamed in. The oohs and ahhs continued along with the picture taking and questions. Raymond and Fred made sure the line kept moving, and all was going smoothly.

At about 10:45 Fred grabbed an officer standing just outside the memorial and asked him to please come inside and help Raymond move people along in a timely fashion. Fred left to meet Governor Brad Shear and Economic Development Secretary Helen O'Malley. Just as he arrived at the back of the court house where reserved parking spaces had been set up, a large, black Suburban escorted by a Kentucky State Police car pulled into the reserved spaces. The governor got out of the Suburban and opened the door for Secretary O'Malley. Driving the Kentucky State Police escort car was officer Ape Cornett. Ape had previously been a deputy for Sheriff Sterling, but had resigned in order to pursue a career with the Kentucky State Police. It was his resignation that permitted Bert to hire Kyle Potter after he completed school at Eastern Kentucky State University's Law Enforcement Program.

"Governor and Madame Secretary, welcome once again to Harlan. It is our genuine pleasure to have you in our fair city today," said Mayor Fred Knapp with a big smile.

"Our pleasure Mr. Mayor," Governor Shear replied. "I just hope things are a little quieter this year than they were for our gathering last year."

"I know they will be, Governor," Fred replied. "And it means a lot to us for you to be here as well Madame Secretary."

"Thank you, mayor," said Helen O'Malley. "The pleasure is all mine. I always enjoy visiting Harlan . . . it's a beautiful little town."

"Hey Fred, good to see you," shouted Ape Cornett as he exited his police cruiser.

"Ape, it's always a pleasure having you back here in Harlan. Thanks for bringing the Governor and Secretary," Fred replied.

"Like a homecoming for me, Mr. Mayor," Ape replied.

Fred then said, "I think everything is all ready for your viewing. If you'll be so kind as to follow me we'll get you right in the memorial." They began walking from the back of the court house to the memorial.

When they approached the long line waiting to get into the memorial the politicians did what politicians do .... they started shaking hands with everyone in line. The media came running and started taking pictures. It was another twenty minutes before they got through shaking hands with everyone in line and arrived at the memorial. They then were escorted inside the building and it was cleared of the public to enable the Governor and Secretary to spend about fifteen minutes viewing the anchor cross and talking with both Randy and Felix. The media were allowed in also to get photographs and television footage. After the fifteen minutes allotted, Fred then asked the media to please exit and he escorted the Governor and Secretary back to their car. Appropriate good-byes were said. Ape Cornett escorted the Suburban back out of Harlan and the mayor returned to the memorial, satisfied that all had gone exactly as planned this time. The mayor then relieved the officer standing in for him in the memorial, and resumed working with Raymond to move the public viewing line along.

•••

All continued to go smoothly, until about 2:30 pm when a fellow wearing a thread-bare sport coat and a wide brimmed hat pulled down over his eyes entered the memorial. Kyle eyed him suspiciously, but did not immediately recognize him. From the other end of the line Bert saw him enter through the metal detector, and also became a little suspicious, but like Kyle did not recognize him. About the time the man got directly in front of the anchor cross screams could be heard outside the memorial. Kyle immediately left his station to look outside to see what was going on. Bert remained to keep guard on the anchor cross.

When Kyle raced outside through the South entrance door he saw a very unusual sight. There, in plain view of everyone, was ole Bennie, the town drunk, with his pants and shorts pulled down around his ankles and he was bent over pointing his rear quarters toward all those standing in line. Two elderly ladies had apparently fainted after screaming, and two officers had rushed to their aid. Many of the men in line were laughing and pointing toward Bennie's bare bottom. Other ladies waiting in line just gazed with astonished looks on their faces. Still others held their hands over their eyes. Kyle rushed up to Bennie and grabbed his shorts and pants and pulled them up. The smell of whiskey was overwhelming. Ole Bennie was drunk as a skunk. Kyle finally got his pants buttoned and was looking to locate another officer to take Bennie to jail when he heard yet another commotion coming from inside the memorial.

Badass had managed to position himself directly in front of Sheriff Sterling. When the screaming started outside, he reached his right hand around toward his rear pocket as though he was trying to reach his handkerchief, and then extended it up toward the middle of his back and felt the valve. He then started extending his left hand to point the nozzle directly toward the sheriff's head. Bert got a frown on his face, trying to understand what this guy was up to. Badass then turned the valve releasing the sulfuric acid to pass into the tubing attached to the nozzle.

Bert's senses were on high alert. He had the strong intuitive feeling that the guy standing before him raising his arm was about to do something that would harm the Helena Anchor Cross. His reflex response was to lean forward and place both arms around the cabinet containing the anchor cross and pull it tightly against his chest. Just as he did this he noticed that the person in front of him had his left arm fully extended pointed at his head. It was then that he saw a stream of liquid squirting from some kind of nozzle in the fellow's coat sleeve, and the liquid was coming directly at his face! Two things then happened that Bert would remember for the rest of his life, but never be able to fully understand. Just as the stream got within an inch of his eyes it was somehow diverted downward and splashed harmlessly on the floor. At the same time Bert looked at the Helena Anchor Cross and saw a very strange thing. Coming from the wooden side of the cross there was a wisp of smoke, apparently caused from the golden anchor cross being hot. The smoke formed in the shape of a long inverted teardrop, with a single dot of smoke below it. It looked exactly like an explanation point! And then the smoke suddenly began to change both form and color. It changed its form from an explanation point into a cross, and its color changed to blood red. Then, in the twinkling of an eye, the smoke vanished. The mysterious power of the anchor cross had been demonstrated once more, and this time, with the smoke signals, it was as though it had talked to Bert.

The problem for Badass started after he opened the valve. A bit of the acid flowed as intended toward the Sheriff's face, but suddenly the spot where the tubing was attached to the valve came loose. Instead of the acid flowing into the tubing it started to pour down Badass's rear quarters and on down his pants to his shoes. Smoke started to come from his pants and shoes. He started screaming and tried to run for the exit door, but Bert ran around the end of the counter and grabbed him before he could get out. Fortunately, there was a fire extinguisher hanging on the wall next to the exit door. Bert grabbed it and started to spray Badass's pants and shoes. Unfortunately, the spray from the fire extinguisher forced some of the acid onto Badass's skin, causing louder and shriller screams. Bert continued to spray him with the extinguisher, not knowing what else to do. Kyle and two other officers came running back into the memorial and over to help Bert. Kyle saw the holes that had formed in both Badass's pants and shoes and immediately called for medics. Fortunately, there was a team of two stationed just outside the memorial. They came in and examined Badass as he continued to scream and curse. By injecting him with a strong sedative they were able to get him calmed down, onto a stretcher, and then headed to the hospital.

Standing in the crowd close to the doughboy watching all the activity was Eagle Eye Looney. When he saw Bennie start to moon all those in line, he thought everything was going to go exactly as planned. Unfortunately for him, the next thing he saw was Badass being taken out of the memorial on a stretcher. Eagle Eye's next thought was that it was probably time for him to relocate. He headed for his pick-up truck.

After another fifteen minutes to clean up all the mess in the memorial, and to get those in line outside calmed down after Bennie's mooning, the Helena Anchor Cross viewing continued. The rest of day went smoothly until closing at 8 pm. Everyone then sighed a big breath of relief, and headed home. It had been quite a day.

Chapter 36

⁓

Harlan, Kentucky

The morning worship service at New Hope Baptist Church in Harlan had been filled to capacity ever since Pastor Raymond Bell returned from his mission trip to the Seychelles. Each Sunday he would share some of those experiences with the congregation. He could recall every single profession of faith. He always took the time after each mission service to talk with those making decisions, and to try to learn a bit about them and their station in life. These made wonderful stories to share with his congregation, and they were always well received. This morning was special. He had Felix Faure, the owner of the plantation on Mahe Island where he discovered the Helena Anchor Cross, sitting in the front row, along with Dr. Randy Peters and all of their Harlan friends. The congregation knew that Mr. Faure and Dr. Peters would be there and share time with Pastor Bell in the pulpit this morning. Yesterday's highly successful viewing of the Helena Anchor Cross greatly enhanced anticipation for their comments this morning.

Raymond had shortened his sermon in order to leave time for the comments from Mr. Faure and Dr. Peters. At the conclusion of his sermon an invitational hymn was sung and two people responded by accepting Christ. Raymond then said, "My friends, we have already been blessed beyond measure today by the two new Christians in our presence. I know you are also aware of the presence this morning of Mr. Faure and Dr. Peters. They have graciously agreed to share some thoughts with us."

Raymond then reached under his gown and pulled out the Helena Anchor Cross that hung about his neck. He held it up for all to see, and rotated it 360 degrees to let everyone see both the beautiful golden and wooden sides. Every eye in the congregation was open wide, and every face exhibited a look of awe. Smiles of understanding were evident on all. Raymond then said, "Folks, this anchor cross truly needs no introduction. I know that each of you are well aware that the side with the gold was cast by Constantine the Great around 325 A.D. using gold that could be traced back to the start of the church and was blessed by Jesus Christ. The side with the wood was then carved from a piece of the True Cross discovered by Constantine's mother, Helena, in 326 A.D. in Jerusalem, and the two sides were then joined together." Tears rolled down Raymond's face as he held and looked at the anchor cross. "I am so grateful that Mr. Felix Faure, the owner of the Helena Anchor Cross, permitted it to be brought to Harlan for viewing, and equally grateful to Dr. Randy Peters for all his assistance and research to define and understand this wonderful artifact. So now I'm going to ask each of them to share a few thoughts with you."

Felix Faure then stood and walked to the podium. Felix and Raymond shook hands, and Raymond returned the anchor cross under his gown.

Felix then said, "My friends, my name is Felix Faure. I am a native of the Seychelles, where I operate a plantation that I inherited from my forefathers. The plantation originally began operation around 1820 by Jean-Paul Faure, and I represent the 6th generation that followed. Two gentleman named only Red and Bones drifted ashore at the plantation in 1860 after their ship sank in a terrible storm. Red was wearing the Helena Anchor Cross that Pastor Bell just showed you. Jean-Paul Faure kept a very detailed diary, and from it we learned how the anchor cross found its way to the plantation. There is a chapel on the plantation and Jean-Paul placed the beautiful anchor cross in a display case in that chapel. But until Pastor Bell saw it, no one knew anything about it other than its history back to Red and Bones. Then after Dr. Peters came to see it and discussed with me what he thought was its likely origin, I readily agreed for him to bring it back here to Kentucky for further study. That was a really good decision, if I do say so myself! Dr. Peters has established its identity beyond any doubt. So just allow me to thank you good people of Harlan for all the wonderful hospitality. I had looked forward greatly to visiting here, and the beauty and friendship I found far exceeded my expectations. Thank you for listening to me, and now I'd like Dr. Peters to share some of his thoughts."

Felix then shook hands with Randy as he approached the podium. Felix walked back to his seat, and Randy said, "Mr. Faure is truly a jewel. The Helena Anchor Cross is priceless, yet he allowed me to bring it to Kentucky for study. Not many people would have made that decision. And now It's my pleasure to be able to announce another absolutely astounding decision made by Mr. Faure. Because he is convinced that this Savior's Cross was intended by Helena to be on display in the Church of the Holy Sepulchre in Jerusalem, and because it found its way to his plantation after being stolen from that church, he has decided that after I have completed my study with it at the Center for Appalachian Research it will be returned to the Church of the Holy Sepulchre for permanent display."

Although applause is not common in Baptist churches, it immediately broke out upon the announcement and continued for several minutes. Felix Faure shyly walked back to the podium and waved to everyone with a big smile. Raymond then joined the two at the podium, and all three began waving and smiling at the applauding audience. Raymond again pulled out the Helena Anchor Cross and held it high. The applause went up about ten decibels!

After the applause finally died down Raymond said, "So how was that for a morning worship service! Thanks so much to Mr. Faure and Dr. Peters for being with us this morning, and thanks to each of you for your presence. Let us now have a closing prayer and we shall adjourn."

•••

Betty Bell had invited the friends over to her home after church. She had prepared sandwiches and salad. After the meal everyone retired to the living room to talk about all the activities of the past couple of days.

Fred began, "Folks, I know each of you likely saw what I did on the television news last evening. It's not real often that Harlan makes the lead network story, especially with good news! When I saw the screen fill with the image of the Helena Anchor Cross I knew that good things would follow, and I wasn't disappointed. They showed lots of shots of downtown Harlan, interviews with Governor Shear, Secretary O'Malley, Felix, and Randy, and they even carried my ugly face welcoming them to the city. I'm just overjoyed that they had left by the time ole Bennie and Badass Brown did their things ..... that would have spoiled everything."

"Speaking of that," said Raymond, "did anyone see anything of Eagle Eye Looney? He had to be involved in all that."

Kyle spoke up, "I caught a glimpse of his old pick-up truck driving away, but didn't see him anywhere around the memorial."

Bert then said, "Certainly I don't know anything for sure, but I'm betting that the botched attempt by Badass to spray me with acid was the last straw for Eagle Eye. Whoever put out the contract on me will be looking for him, and while he's not the brightest of our citizens I bet he's got enough sense to get out of Dodge and try and become invisible. I'd be shocked to see him around these parts again."

"I'd agree with that," Kyle replied. "My guess would be that he'll be going just about as far as his old pick-up will take him."

Randy then asked, "Sheriff, have you heard any news about the two would be robbers that stopped Felix and me on Friday?"

"Some," Bert said. "Since bullet wounds have to be reported, I've been checking all around for anything that fits. I noticed that a hospital at Prestonsburg treated two men on Friday evening for bullet wounds. One had a bullet in the leg, the other in his rear. Moreover, the guy with the rear-end lead had a severe burn to his right hand. The guy with the leg wound was a fellow named Big Jim Owens . . . he's a notorious drug dealer up in Floyd County. The other fellow was Mad Mike Hatfield. He's one of Big Jim's flunkies. I think beyond doubt they were the two, but proving it would be very difficult. I'm sure they lined up alibi's before they went to the hospital. If we could have caught them here in Harlan County we could likely have made a good case against them, but unless you two want to try and press charges I think we should just thank the good Lord that they were the only ones that got hurt."

Felix spoke up, "I agree with you Bert, I'm sure we could pick them out of a lineup, but they would likely still go free when their witnesses swore to false stories. We weren't harmed, thanks to the Helena Anchor Cross, and it'd be my vote to just forget it."

Randy nodded in agreement and said, "I'll vote that way as well. Let's just be thankful that everything turned out fine for us. With their physical injuries they'll suffer some, and the loss of the two million dollars they were counting on will pain them a lot more. Let's just let it go at that."

Bert and Kyle nodded in agreement.

Randy then said, "We talked about Eagle Eye. What about Bennie and Badass?"

Bert said, "Bennie is in our jail trying to sober up. I'll likely let him out later this afternoon. I feel certain he was just doing what he was told to do by Eagle Eye and Badass. His little 'mooning' episode was just to create a distraction for Badass. They probably just gave him a bottle of booze to do it."

"I hate to say this," replied Kyle, "but it was funny. When I went charging out of the memorial to see what was going on, there stood ole Bennie with his pants down around his ankles, bent over and mooning everyone in the line. Ladies were fainting, men were laughing, and ole Bennie was just about so drunk he was ready to fall over."

Fred then asked, "What about Badass Brown. Have you heard from the hospital?"

"Yeah, I called them early this morning to check on him," Bert replied. "He'll be in there a while. He has a lot of acid burns on his rear quarters, his legs, and even some on his feet. That sulfuric acid is really bad news. The hospital said that the worse burns were on his buttocks. I'm not trying to be funny here, but he's certainly lived up to his name!"

Everyone laughed and Fred said, "Badass for sure now. I'll have to cut that picture out of the **Enterprise** that shows him headed for the ambulance on a stretcher and post it on my wall at Creech Cafe. When people ask about it I'll really have a whopper of a story to tell!"

Raymond then said, "Folks, I would just like to say again how indebted we are to Mr. Faure here for making all this possible. Like the rest of you, I'm sure, Betty and I have certainly enjoyed greatly meeting you Felix, and commend you for your decision to place the Helena Anchor Cross back in its rightful place in Jerusalem."

"Thank you Raymond," Felix replied. "It was really an easy decision. I couldn't have done anything else. Thank you, Betty, and all you fine new friends for being so hospitable toward me. I'll always remember each of you, and Harlan, very fondly. Randy and I will discuss some of the details about the final arrangements for the Helena Anchor Cross on our way back to Lexington tomorrow morning, and then I leave to go back home tomorrow evening. It has been a great trip for me, one I'll never forget. Pax Tecum!"